Christine Pullein-Thompson has been involved with horses all her life—she opened a riding school with her sisters when she was fourteen. She started writing at fifteen and published her first book with her sisters Diana and Josephine. Christine has written more than 90 books which have been translated into nine languages. She is best known for her pony books but has also written the highly successful Jessie series about a dog and general fiction stories for younger readers.

Christine has four children and lives with her husband Julian Popescu in a moated Parsonage in Suffolk with two horses, a dog and a cat.

Other Pony Books by Christine Pullein-Thompson

Published by *Cavalier Paperbacks*

A Pony In Distress
Stolen Ponies
The Lost Pony
For Want of A Saddle

I RODE A WINNER

Christine Pullein-Thompson

CAVALIER
PAPERBACKS

© Christine Pullein-Thompson 1994

Published by Cavalier Paperbacks 1994
PO Box 1821, Warminster, Wilts BA12 0YD

Cover Design by Michelle Bellfield
Cover Photograph by Alistair Fyfe
Courtesy of The Infantry Saddle Club, Warminster

ISBN 1–899470–02–6

Typeset in New Century Schoolbook and Ottawa
by Ann Buchan (Typesetters), Shepperton
Printed and bound by
Cox and Wyman, Reading, Berkshire

CHAPTER ONE

It isn't easy to watch your parents part. I missed most of the rows, because I was sent to boarding school and when I returned they had already separated. I sat in my bedroom staring at my china horses. I didn't see them because I was imagining my father leaving, banging the front door behind him, going without bothering to say goodbye to me, to leave a note explaining. It hurt. Then slowly tears came. Sometime later I was aware of my mother in the room, tall and beautiful, waving a letter.

"Simon wants to have you for the summer," she said. "He says you'll have to work for your living. But you don't mind, do you? There are sixteen horses in, at the moment and some others turned out."

Simon is my brother. He failed most of his A levels and then, against everybody's advice, married Tina. He had been riding for some time and Tina was already running a stable, so they simply moved into the stud groom's cottage and ran it together. He's years older than I am. I remembered him coming him from school, cursing like a trooper, playing his radio full volume until the rest of the household reached screaming point.

"Do you think we'll get on?" I asked now. "I mean we never did, did we?"

"He's changed, mellowed, and Tina's a sweety," replied Mum. "Anyway, there really isn't anywhere else to go. We're selling this house and I'm off tomorrow to stay in London and you know you would be bored there the whole holidays."

I was pleased that I did not have to make up my mind.

"You can come to me later, or stay with Dad, whichever you like: I shall give you some money and Tina will help you get any clothes you may need—jeans, jodhpurs, etc . . . You'll have to learn to muck out and muck in," said Mum laughing.

I remembered Tina at her wedding. She had arrived and left in a coach drawn by a four-in-hand.

"Dad and I will be keeping in touch," continued Mum. "Dad wants you for Easter and you're definitely coming to me for Christmas."

I started to feel like a parcel, something wrapped up in brown paper waiting to be posted somewhere for Christmas. I was trying not to cry again.

"You've always wanted to ride," said Mum sounding guilty for the first time. "This is your big chance, darling."

"Yes, I'm sure it will be great," I replied. "I shall enjoy every moment. I shall be a good worker and earn my keep."

But I didn't mean it, for suddenly I wasn't sure of anything any more. My whole life seemed to be toppling about my ears. I wanted Mum to leave my room, but she lingered picking things up and putting them down again.

"You will understand everything when you are

6

older," she said at last, putting an arm round my shoulder.

"I'm sure I will," I replied, "even Dad leaving without saying goodbye."

"He's writing to Simon's place. Why don't you change into a dress and we'll go out and have tea somewhere," said Mum.

We lived in a town. My riding had been done during the summer holidays at a trekking centre in Wales. Outside the streets were full of people and we had to wait ages for tea. I kept biting my nails while Mum made bright conversation.

Next day Simon came in a Land Rover to pick me up. I hadn't seen him for nearly a year and he had changed. He seemed much happier and he had left his radio at home. His shoulders were wider too and his hair bleached yellow by the sun.

My cases were ready packed. I had put on jeans and a yellow shirt.

Mum fussed over Simon and made him coffee in the kitchen which would soon belong to someone else. I stood on the pavement saying goodbye to everything. The garden was full of roses. A bird was washing himself in the bird bath on the lawn. I felt faintly sick.

Simon came outside at last. "Tina can't wait for you to come," he said taking the two cases which held all my belongings. "She's got rows of ponies lined up for you to ride. You're going to have a wonderful time."

He put the cases in the Land Rover. I climbed in after them.

"I keep telling Debbie she's in for a great time," said Mum.

I wanted to leave at once. I hate partings and this one was even worse than usual. It was like parting from my whole childhood.

"We'll look after her," said Simon climbing into the Land Rover.

"I'll write every day," promised Mum, while Simon started the Land Rover. "And I'll ring up tonight to see how you are, Debbie."

I thought of someone else sleeping in my bedroom.

"Goodbye," I shouted without looking at anyone. "I shall be all right." My voice had a croak in it. I looked straight ahead along the road and saw that the milkman was delivering milk and that the postman was late as usual.

"It's best to get away," said Simon after a time in an embarrassed voice. "I found that out quite soon."

"But I'm younger than you were," I said.

"You'll like the ponies," continued Simon, "and there are a couple of foals in the lower paddock. I hope to ride at Badminton next year."

"You mean compete there?" I asked.

Simon nodded. "I shall probably break my neck, but one has to progress," he said. "And then there's the Olympics in three years' time . . . ."

He made everything seem possible. We were nearly out of the town now, green fields stretched into the distance.

"Surely you and Tina don't look after all those horses on your own," I said.

"Gosh no, there's Derek; he's our working pupil,

you'll like him, everyone does ... Then there's Rosalind, Rosie for short. We all work very hard."

"I've never mucked out, you'll have to show me how," I said.

I was feeling better—rather as though I had just woken up from a nightmare and found none of it was true after all. "There's some chocolate in that bag, help yourself," said Simon stopping at some traffic lights.

Another five minutes and we were in the country, driving through a valley with hills sprinkled with trees on each side.

"Only another thirty miles," said Simon.

"How was school? Are you glad to be leaving."

"I don't know yet, some of it was fun," I answered. "I expect I shall miss my friends."

I found it difficult to keep my eyes open. I had hardly slept for two nights. "It is better for people to part if they are unhappy," said Simon. "You couldn't expect our parents to stay together for another five years just because of you."

"I know that. It just took me by surprise," I answered.

The verges were white with meadowsweet. Cows stood sleepily in fields. I think I slept. Sometime later Simon touched my shoulder.

"We are nearly there, just three more minutes," he said, and I knew by his voice that he loved every inch of the road and that this was home to him as nowhere else had ever been before.

"There are the brood mares. Look! Over there," he cried. "Under the elms."

I rubbed the sleep from my eyes and saw two ponies standing by a water trough.

"They're called Nutmeg and Cinnamon," Simon told me. "They're ordinary ponies, but in foal to very good stallions."

"When will they foal?"

"Next June."

It seemed a long time away to me at that moment.

"Here we are," said Simon driving into a yard.

A crowd was waiting for us. "Welcome to Bullrock Stables," they shouted.

"Come and be introduced," said Simon leaping out of the Land Rover.

Rows of horses' heads watched us over loose-box doors. Two Jack Russell terriers yapped wildly with excitement and then threw themselves at Simon.

"Tina, Rosie and Derek, this is my sister Debbie," announced Simon.

Rosie held out her hand.

"I'm glad you're light," said Tina, "you'll be able to exercise some of the ponies. I had awful visions of you weighing ten stone."

"I'm not much of a rider unfortunately," I answered shaking Rosie's hand.

Tina was slim with long dark hair and blue eyes. Rosie was well built with ruddy cheeks and a ready laugh. Derek had brown hair which didn't lie flat and serious brown eyes. He was taller than I was, but not as tall as Simon who is six foot. They all had a healthy look about them.

"Come on in," said Tina. "Our place is small and untidy."

Derek carried my cases. My bedroom was at the back. It was a small peaceful room with old fashioned windows and walls more than a foot thick. The floor sloped and there was a beam across the middle of the ceiling which you had to duck under.

There was one large untidy sitting room downstairs, which you walked straight into, and a kitchen with a Raeburn cooker installed, and a larder. The bathroom was at the back made out of the old wash house. Derek slept outside in a room adjoining the stables. The rooms all needed painting but the whole place was wonderfully comfortable with an atmosphere of peace about it. "Do you want to telephone your mother?" asked Tina when she had shown me round, only omitting to show me Simon's and her bedroom which she said was in shambles and unfit to be seen by anyone, even relations.

"Perhaps I had better," I said. I dialled home. Mum was still there.

"I've arrived. I like it," I said. "Are you all right?"

"I knew you'd love it," replied Mum cheerfully.

"I'm just packing. The removal men are going to be here at any moment."

Our furniture was going into storage. I could see my face in a gilt framed mirror as I talked. My mouse-brown hair was tangled, my brown eyes were red from crying, my skin looked pale, my cheeks flabby. It wasn't a face I liked at that moment.

"Well, be seeing you then," I said.

"Here they are. I must go. Look after yourself," said Mum. "Don't fall off."

"Who are they?"

"The removal men."

I didn't want to say goodbye. I was suddenly homesick. I saw myself failing at everything, falling off the ponies, getting tonsillitis, as I often did, and then no-one nursing me. I saw myself tongue-tied at lunch and miserable at supper and Tina and Simon becoming tired of me. I had never been a success at school; never a success at anything.

All this went through my mind as Mum said, "Goodbye darling," and hung up.

I looked round the room and wondered how long I would stay. I didn't want any lunch but Tina made me eat.

"You can't ride on an empty stomach," she said.

"I'm no good at riding," I answered.

"Don't be absurd," said Simon. "Of course you can ride."

"I've caught up Heather for you. She belongs to an old lady called Mrs Wells. She's a very sensible pony," said Tina. "She has to be exercised several times a week."

"Or she gets laminitis," added Derek.

"Laminitis?"

"Otherwise called pony gout," replied Derek, leaving me none the wiser.

We ate mushroom omelettes with saute potatoes, followed by ice cream.

"I have to take out Charlatan," said Simon, leaving the table. "Will you lunge Dauntless, Derek? He needs about twenty five minutes, a little longer on the near rein than the off."

"And don't forget that the blacksmith is coming at

12

three o'clock to shoe Trampus and Rocket," said Tina.

"I'll wash up," I offered. "I like being by myself and you seem to have a lot to do."

"Rosie can manage the blacksmith," said Simon over his shoulder, as he left the room followed by Spick and Span. "But I want Trampus to have wedges behind, don't forget now."

I suppose to them it was just any other day, but to me it was like moving into a strange country. I didn't talk their language nor was I like them. I was pale and indecisive. They were sunburnt and knew where they were going. They left the table with long strides. They didn't hesitate or stop to wonder whether they were saying the right thing; even Derek at sixteen was self-assured.

"Don't wash up. We'll do it later," said Tina, clearing the table. "Put on riding clothes and come and try Heather. Fresh air will do you good."

I changed slowly, listening to Simon whistling as he led a chestnut horse out of a loose-box and mounted him. He saw my face at the window and waved.

"Come and ride," he yelled as though offering me a treat. "Don't mope in the house all afternoon."

I remembered him at home on long summer days, driving everyone mad, running away with my toys to hide them in the garden. I was five then and I hated him.

He had changed beyond all recognition. Perhaps I will change, I thought, putting on my skull-cap. Perhaps I'll become a marvellous rider and surprise everyone. I ran down the narrow cottage stairs which

13

had no carpet. Spick and Span were back in the sitting room lying in the armchairs looking as though they owned the place.

Tina was waiting outside holding a dun pony already tacked up.

"I thought you were never coming," she said.

The blacksmith was shoeing Trampus, a large roan with a Roman nose. Derek was lunging the black thoroughbred, Dauntless, in one of the paddocks. He was completely in control looking like an expert.

I couldn't imagine myself ever catching them up. I patted Heather's short dun neck. "She's sweet," I said. "Shall I pull up the girths. Do I need a stick?"

And I thought, no I shall never make it. I've started too late.

CHAPTER TWO

I rode Heather in the schooling paddock. She was quiet and well behaved. Tina stood in the middle telling me how to sit, shouting "Heels down, shorten your reins, sit up, you're not a sack of potatoes."

It was quite different from riding at the trekking centre when the ponies had followed each other on well-worn tracks. Now I had to steer Heather, to coordinate my movements; it wasn't easy. I started to sense Tina's despair. She had hoped I could ride. Now she found herself saddled with another beginner.

"That's enough for today," she said. "Tomorrow we'll hack. I'll put you on the leading rein and you can practise rising without holding on to the saddle."

Tina showed me how to untack Heather. Then she led me, riding bareback, to the field behind the stables.

"You'll soon learn," she said sounding unconvinced.

I watched the blacksmith after that, and Rosie gave me a sweet and said, "Don't look so glum. You can't be worse than I am. I'm just hopeless. They only keep me because I muck out, and most girls won't."

She stood sucking sweets while I walked up and down like a tiger in a cage biting my nails until the blacksmith said, "You'll never get fat that's certain, not the way you keep going up and down. What's the matter?" He rubbed his hands on his leather apron and looked at me properly for the first time.

"What's eating you?" he asked.

"Nothing, nothing at all," I answered.

Derek was rugging up Dauntless.

"Mucking out time," he said briskly. "We only go round with a skip this time. The real mucking out is done at six thirty in the morning."

"Six thirty?" I said.

"That's right."

He fetched a big wicker basket and showed me how to pick up the droppings and shake the straw.

Then Simon was back riding into the yard on Charlatan and Tina was paying the blacksmith while Rosie rushed to the cottage to put the kettle on for tea.

"You can fill up the buckets," Derek said, "pour out the dirty water. Look, here's the tap," he was talking to me as though I was an imbecile. I moved so slowly compared to the rest of them and when a bucket was full of water I could hardly lift it.

I could see the veiled impatience in his eyes. "You can turn the tap on faster than that," he said. "We'll never get done at this rate."

Rosie brought us all mugs of tea; then she started filling up hay-nets, weighing each one on the scales in the barn. Tina was in the saddle room cleaning the tack. Simon started mixing up feeds. "Hurry up with the water, Debbie," he called. "I can't feed until they are all watered."

Rosie helped me. "They haven't any hearts around

16

here," she said. "You're from a town, aren't you?"

I nodded. She gave me a polo mint. "You fetch the empties and I'll fill them," she said. "Don't let them upset you. . ."

At last the feeding was done. Then we all moved into the saddle room to help Tina with the tack. "Only three more days to the Horse Trials," she said.

"We'll have to stay here Derek, because Captain Peters is coming to ride Mainspring. He's competing in the Horse Trials on the next day. Rosie will stay and help. Debbie can come with us."

"Okay," said Derek. "I'll have Mainspring ready as usual."

"And there's a man from Devon coming to look at some of the young horses tomorrow with a view to selling them in Europe," she continued.

"For horse meat?" I asked.

"Of course not. For jumpers. The chestnut should fetch four thousand at least," said Tina.

"I'll catch them early," offered Rosie.

I watched the others cleaning tack until Derek threw me a duster and said, "you can polish the stirrups. It's rude to stand and watch others working."

"Don't bully her," retorted Rosie. "Give her time to settle down."

The day was nearly over. It seemed to have passed very quickly. Rosie left at five and we all wandered indoors soon after.

My arms and legs were aching and I went straight to my room because I wanted to be alone to think things over. I looked out of my window and the trees were casting shadows on the hills and I could hear a cow lowing in the distance. Otherwise there was a silence and I was not accustomed to silence, so I unpacked my Walkman, speakers and cassettes and sat listening to 'Take That' until Simon banged on my door and shouted, "Can you turn it down a bit? I want to telephone. How about giving Tina a hand with supper? I've got to go out in a minute to get some oats . . ."

"All right," I answered. But I didn't help Tina with the supper. I switched off my Walkman, lay back on my bed and in less than a minute I was asleep.

The next morning I was so stiff I could hardly move.

Tina called me at ten minutes past six with a cup of tea. Outside birds were singing and in the distance cocks were crowing and the sun was just rising over the misty dew-drenched fields.

"I can't move. I'm stiff. It hurts me to turn my head," I groaned.

"There's sugar in the saucer. We'll expect you outside in about fifteen minutes. Okay?" asked Tina.

"No, I'm too stiff."

"That will soon go." She was still in a dressing gown and her hair was uncombed. She looked quite different than she did in riding clothes; more fragile. I wondered where all her strength came from.

I could hear her running downstairs, calling to Derek to get a move on. The tea tasted strong. Outside the horses were whinnying and I could hear Simon talking to them, saying " Steady there, your turn next." And the banging of impatient hoofs on doors, the rattle of feed-bins and the trundling of a wheelbarrow. I had never been up so early before. I looked out of the window and now the sun was breaking through the trees dissolving the muslin cobwebs which joined the meadowsweet together. I forgot my stiff neck as I dressed. I ran downstairs and out into the yard.

"Hurray," shouted Tina. "Here's our new stable hand . . ."

Derek handed me a fork. "She had better start with Misty," Tina said.

Misty was an old grey pony. He didn't work any more. this was his last home and his owner paid £10 a week for it.

"You can turn him out first. Here, I'll help," offered Rosie. "He stays out till the flies drive him mad, then he comes in. He's thirty."

It took me nearly an hour to muck out the box. Derek had done five by the time I had finished, and they all looked better than mine . . .

Tina called us into a breakfast of bacon and eggs, toast and coffee.

"You're doing very well," she said. "We'll make a horsewoman of you yet."

"Without a doubt," agreed Simon.

I knew they were only being kind, but I felt pleased just the same. "I'll muck out two tomorrow, if it kills me," I said. . . .

I rode all morning, first on Heather, then on a bay called Searchlight. Derek disappeared with Simon to jump some young horses over the cross-country course. Then we all met again for elevens consisting of mugs of tea and bread and cheese. Later two strange men appeared and spent the rest of the morning looking over the young horses. Rosie and I did the lunch feeding together and she told me that she was one of seven children and the only one interested in horses.

Later, after lunch, I wandered round the horses trying to learn which was which. The stables were shaped in an arc and built in brick with Staffordshire brick floors and slate tiled roofs. There were twelve such loose-boxes and a high ceilinged tack room with a small boiler in it. Behind was a row of wooden boxes where the ponies lived.

I knew Searchlight of course. He was fifteen hands with a star and was being looked after while his owner was in France. I knew dun Heather too and Mainspring who was grey with darker points, and a nose which twitched hopefully when one passed his box. And of course, I knew Charlatan with a strip of white on his face, two white socks behind and a mane the colour of Devonshire cream. But the horse I liked best was a neat grey mare. She carried herself like a princess. She was half Arab and always looking for excitement. She had been in the stables for nearly a month and was now waiting for a buyer. Tina called her a girl's ride, but no-one had appeared capable of handling her so far. Her asking price was three thousand pounds. I sympathised with the mare's restless spirit. I was sure she felt trapped in the loose-box. She needed wide open spaces, a chance to stretch her neat grey legs, the wind whistling through her mane. She was called Cleopatra, Cleo for short.

In the evening, Tina gave me a book to read. It was called THE NOVICE'S BOOK OF FIRST AID AND STABLE MANAGEMENT. "You'll learn a lot from this," she said.

Inside there were drawings of fearsome wounds, a picture of a horse in slings and much useful advice. "Tomorrow I'll teach you how to bandage," promised Tina. "And the next day we go to the horse trials."

I was settling down and beginning to be ambitious. I wanted to ride in horse trials, to be someone like Simon.

I was up first in the morning. I put on the kettle and ran down to the stables. Everywhere birds were singing. The horses looked at me and whinnied. Everything seemed new and untouched in the early morning light.

"Gosh, You've beaten us all!" cried Simon coming out of the cottage. "Aren't you amazed at yourself?"

I nodded because I was. I couldn't understand how I had managed to be first, to be up with the dawn and enjoying it.

Later, Derek taught me to lunge. "You make a V," he said. "With you and the whip and the horse, and you don't stand still, you follow the horse making your own smaller circle. Look, like this."

Next, Tina taught me how to bandage, and the difference between exercise and stable bandages. Then Rosie gave me a grooming lesson. And afterwards I rode Searchlight again. In the evening we cleaned Charlatan's tack together in the tack room polishing every buckle, and I could feel the air of excitement growing as the trailer was bedded down, the plaiting things put ready, and Charlatan's white socks washed and bandaged. A sack of feed was put into the Land Rover. A net of hay hung in the groom's compartment.

Rosie went home, saying, "Best of luck Simon if I don't see you in the morning."

Charlatan was given a late feed. Simon went through the dressage test for the last time with Tina. We listened to the weather forecast. Tina set her alarm clock for four thirty and put out the picnic things.

"I'll wake you at six, Debbie," she said.

Simon's boots were polished in the sitting room, his coat hung on a coat-hanger, his helmet with its silk cover waited in a chair. Even the dogs felt the air of excitement and sat listening for intruders, their ears pricked.

We retired to bed early. I read about Tetanus, otherwise called Lockjaw for a bit; then tried to put a tourniquet on my arm. I could hear Simon going round the stables for the last time, and the sound of a horse getting up to greet him. Then everything was still and silent.

CHAPTER THREE

The morning was grey. Tina was standing on a bucket plaiting Charlatan when I appeared in the yard.

"Hang on to his head. I've lost three needles already," she yelled.

Simon was hitching the trailer to the Land Rover. Half the loose-boxes were mucked out already. Rosie arrived on a bike.

"Don't let him move, talk to him," said Tina.

Charlatan was on edge, too. His feed was unfinished in the manger and he was sweating under his summer sheet.

"Whoa, steady, calm down," I said.

I knew how he felt. It was like waiting for exams, dreading every minute, so that when at last the moment comes to begin, it is almost a relief.

"You're going to win," I told him. "Everything will be easy. Stop worrying."

Simon's horoscope was good. It said, "Good luck all the way," Tina told me, cutting thread with her teeth.

The air of excitement was infectious. I felt on edge myself. "Finished. Thank you so much," Tina said getting off the bucket.

Charlatan's tack was in the Land Rover now. We

went inside to have breakfast. Simon hardly spoke. Derek came in smelling of the stables. "I hope Rosie isn't going to be ill. She says she feels sick," he said.

"She can't be ill today of all days," said Tina.

Charlatan boxed beautifully. Simon threw up the ramp.

"Good luck," said Derek standing with the terriers in the yard. "We'll keep things going till you're back."

"Don't worry, we won't be late."

It was eight thirty, but it felt much later. The field looked parched in the sunlight and Simon suddenly said, "We've forgotten Charlatan's studs," and we had to turn round and go back.

"Are these your first horse trials?" asked Tina when we were on our way again.

"Yes."

"There's dressage first. Simon's riding at ten o'clock; then there's the cross country. He's down for eleven forty five. The jumping starts at three o'clock."

I looked at my brother. He handled the Land Rover like an old hand; none of the old Simon I remembered, remained. Tina produced a thermos of coffee after we had been on the road for an hour and soon after that we came to a notice which read TO THE TRIALS, and Simon stopped talking. We could hear Charlatan moving restlessly in the trailer as though he, too, knew we were almost there.

Then we reached the summit of a hill and we could see the course laid out below us like a picture. I felt Tina stiffen as she looked at the jumps, and Simon brace himself, as he said, "It's a stiff course, but well within Charlatan's capability."

24

We turned in through a gate and parked the Land Rover.

"You stay here while we walk the course," Tina said. "Just keep talking to Charlatan like you did this morning. It really works." They walked away hand in hand. I climbed into the groom's compartment, and stroked Charlatan's gleaming neck and told him that everything was going to be all right. I heard the first rider being called to the dressage arena, and the sound of ramps being let down and horses being led out into the bright sunshine. I heard someone say, "Simon Ravenswood stands a good chance, if his chestnut will only settle in the dressage." And someone else replied, "He rides too fast for my liking."

The next competitor was called to the dressage arena and all the time I kept talking to Charlatan while he sniffed my hair and relaxed. At last Simon and Tina came back. Tina's face was tense.

Simon said, "It's a smashing course. I don't think much of the pond jump and the coffin jump is enormous, but otherwise ..."

"Take the pond jump slowly or you'll somersault," advised Tina.

We led Charlatan down the ramp, took of his knee caps and leg bandages. We tacked him up and pulled off his tail bandage. I handed Simon his whip, but he said, "Not for the dressage, not the helmet either, just my usual hat."

Then he was in the saddle and riding away and Tina turned to me and said, "I don't like the course. There's a lot of uphill work and Charlatan isn't that

25

fit."

"What about Good luck all the way?" I asked.

"One can't help being afraid sometimes," Tina replied. "And I don't really believe horoscopes, do you?"

"Not really."

Charlatan was very lively. "He's not going to settle," said Tina pessimistically. But when at last he was in the arena and Simon was taking his hat off to the judges, Charlatan seemed to change.

He dropped his nose and arched his neck, and his movements flowed into each other like music. Simon sat very straight, his body hardly moving, so that the whole performance seemed like magic. I could sense Tina's excitement growing.

"It's his best test ever," she cried. "And usually he's bad at dressage."

We watched him bow for the last time. There was a burst of clapping.

"Well done!" cried Tina rushing to meet him.

I led Charlatan up and down, while Simon ate a few sandwiches. The second rider came through the finish of the cross country course. Several people congratulated Simon on his test, and when his marks came up on the board by the secretary's tent, he was leading.

Tina could hardly contain her excitement. Simon screwed studs into Charlatan's shoes; then a man with a grey moustache wearing a checked coat, breeches and boots appeared and said Number 22, are you nearly ready?" Simon put his number on and his helmet and asked for his whip. Tina and I said, "Good luck."

"If he wins this, it will do our business more good than anything else," remarked Tina as he rode away. "We'll be able to ask what we like to school horses. Then we'll be able to have another Rosie and life won't be quite so hard."

We walked to a vantage point where we could see three-quarters of the course. I had a pain in my side now and my heart seemed to be banging my ribs like a sledge hammer.

"He's next," said Tina twisting her hands together. "Was he always so reckless?"

I shook my head. "He was always rather angry," I answered.

"That's because he was bored stiff; there was nothing for him in life then; now it's different . . ." she said.

Simon had started. Tina stood beside me without speaking and I wondered whether she was praying. Her lips moved, but when I listened carefully she was whispering, "Steady, not too fast, push, push on for goodness sake, now steady, easy up the hill." And her body kept moving as though she was riding Charlatan herself.

Number 22, Simon Ravenswood, is over the tiger trap now and going well."

"Thank God," cried Tina.

I was affected too. I walked up and down biting my nails, admiring the way Simon and Charlatan moved together, like something beautiful, which made one think of music. And then he was lost to view.

"There's only the drop fence, the tree trunk and the rustic poles left! He must be all right now," Tina said.

"It's uphill," I pointed out.

We saw him once more and Charlatan seemed to be faltering a little and Tina cried, "Say a prayer for him, Debbie. He's nearly home."

We stood on the hill waiting. Gradually a small crowd collected and someone said, "He should be in sight by now."

"He may have had a stop," said Tina in a small frightened voice.

"Yes, that's probably it," agreed a woman holding two terriers on leads. "His chestnut looked a bit tired as he came up the hill and horses have a wonderful way of stopping when they're tired."

Tina was standing on tiptoe now as though she was trying to see through a window, and her face had gone quite pale.

Then the announcement came bold and clear on the summer air. "Number 22 has fallen at jump eighteen. Will an ambulance go to jump eighteen?" Tina started to run giving shrill cries of anguish while I followed more slowly. The lady with the dogs said, "You'd better go down and take his horse."

"Yes, I'm going," I said, but it wasn't really me speaking, for I was far away now seeing Simon when he was little. I was remembering him riding for the first time long ago in Wales. I remembered the look on his face which had been pure happiness and how he had insisted on untacking his own pony and had talked about nothing else for days. I thought, that was where all this began. A steward met me with Charlatan. I could see people bending over my brother as he lay by the log jump and Tina standing beside him looking small and defenceless.

"Are you his groom?" asked the steward.

"Yes, sort of; I'm his sister."

"Can you manage the horse?"

"Sure."

The steward looked relieved.

Charlatan was soaked with sweat and coated in dust. One of his knees was bleeding.

"It wasn't your fault," I told him. "You did your best . . ."

People were coming back up the hill now. Then the ambulance went by and Tina leaned out to yell, "Try and get home. I'm staying with Simon. I'll telephone."

I shouted back, "How is he?" but she didn't hear.

I heard a man say, "His helmet was split in two."

And another man replied, "The horse wasn't fit, any fool could see that. He went well enough at the beginning and he was nearly home."

"He was leading in the dressage," said someone else. Then a man in a cap appeared and said, "I'm the vet on duty. I think I had better have a look at that knee. Has he been vaccinated against tetanus?"

"I've no idea," I said.

"Isn't there a groom here, someone older with you?"

"There was, there was Tina, his wife, but she's gone with him."

The vet bathed Charlatan's knees, "We'll leave the tetanus injection till you get home; but if he hasn't had one it must be done during the next twenty-four

29

hours," he said, shaking powder on to the wound. "Call your own vet the moment you get back."

I didn't say anything, because I was wondering how I would get back to the stables. The vet looked at me.

"Well, take his saddle off, give him a drink. He needs rubbing down," he shouted before striding away looking furious, while I tied Charlatan to the trailer with his reins and removed his saddle. I found him his headcollar and tried to fathom how I could remove the bridle and replace it with his headcollar without letting him go. At the same time my brain was repeating over and over again the words, "His helmet was split in two." I knew what that meant— a cracked skull.

I summoned all my courage and took off the bridle. Charlatan was marvellous and pushed his nose into the headcollar like an angel. I found a water trough and watered him. After I'd brushed him and rugged him up, I led him into the trailer and gave him a hay-net. The leg bandages were still lying by the Land Rover, where only a few hours ago we had peeled them off so hopefully. It was too late now to put them on again, because I had boxed Charlatan, so I threw them into the Land Rover along with the knee caps and tail bandage. Then I threw up the ramp which was incredibly heavy and turned the screws on it. I was ready to go home now, but, of course, I couldn't drive. I stood and looked around and decided that this was the worst day of my life, and I've had some awful ones, I assure you.

Then, though I'm not religious, I started to pray. I

prayed that Simon would recover completely and that someone would come to drive me home, but for ages nothing happened. I didn't want to watch the other competitors, so I just sat on the ground and thought about life and how depressing it was and that happiness never lasted for long, not even for a few hours. Then a couple came up to me, and said "We've been watching you for ages, dear. Haven't you got anyone to take you home?"

"No. My sister-in-law has gone with my brother. I don't know anything about horses, and here I am," I said, trying to laugh but failing miserably. "I don't know anything. I don't even know if Charlatan's had a tetanus vaccination and, if he hasn't, he needs one before lunch time tomorrow."

"Don't worry, dear," said the lady putting a plump arm round one shoulder. "We know Simon, don't we, Percy? We'll get you home."

Percy braced his shoulders. He was a small man with sideboards and a pipe in his mouth. "That's right. I'll drive you. My wife can follow in the Rover and pick me up. Our daughter has just been round, so with luck we may be back in time to see her over the show jumps."

He checked the ramp and then climbed into the Land Rover.

"I think he's cracked his skull."

"I daresay he has, but so have lots of others, and we're still about," said Percy driving slowly through the gate into the road.

CHAPTER FOUR

We didn't talk much. I was suddenly very tired. Percy told me about his daughter. "She's only fifteen," he said. "And she's already riding with the champs."

"How wonderful," I said.

"Of course, it's cost me a lot, I won't say it hasn't. The one she's riding today cost me twelve thousand pounds."

"All the best things in life cost a lot," I replied suddenly bitter.

"You've said it," agreed Percy.

I thought, I'll never make it. I've started everything too late. I want to be a great rider. But it won't happen, I thought. I'm too weak. I can't even muck out two boxes in an hour yet, or rise at the trot without holding on, and I hated myself. . . .

"You mustn't worry," said Percy, looking at my gloomy face. "Your brother will be all right."

Some time later I slept. Then suddenly we were home and Derek was running to greet us, shouting, "How did you do? Did you get anything?" Then he saw Percy and stopped. "Where's Simon?" he cried, "And Tina? What's happened?"

I had been dreaming and my brain was in a muddle.

32

"Where's my wife?" asked Percy. "She should be here."

The terriers were barking so much it was difficult to hear anything.

"He fell off," I yelled. "He's in hospital. Help me with the ramp."

Rosie came out of a loose-box. "Where's Simon?" she asked.

"For goodness sake, in hospital," I yelled. "We've had a disaster—a frightful disaster," and I was afraid that tears would come to shame me.

Derek backed out Charlatan. His face didn't have any expression on it.

"And Tina, where's Tina?" asked Rosie.

"In hospital with him." I didn't want to talk about it now. The day seemed to have lasted for ever.

Charlatan's box was ready for him. Derek fetched him a mash.

Percy's wife arrived in the Rover. "I went wrong somewhere," she said.

"You'll be all right now?" asked Percy.

I nodded. "I can't thank you enough," I began.

"You do it for someone yourself one day," advised Percy.

"Give Simon our best wishes."

"I will and good luck to your daughter."

Percy's wife patted me on the shoulder. "You're a good girl," she said. "Simon's lucky to have you; you're a treasure."

I didn't know what to say, so I murmured, "Thank you." And then they were gone and all our problems lay ahead, waiting like a mountain to be climbed.

33

Derek started to work on Charlatan. "You didn't do much, he said. "He's still covered with sweat."

"Has he been injected against tetanus?" I asked ignoring Derek's rudeness. "The vet wanted to know."

"Of course, they all have. Don't you know anything?"

"Someone help me with the watering," called Rosie. "I can't do it all on my own."

"I shall have to go in soon. I haven't changed yet, and Tina's going to ring up," I answered.

"I've been ill all day, sick . . . awful," moaned Rosie.

We filled up the buckets together while Derek fussed over Charlatan.

"He's crying. That's why he won't come out and help," Rosie said.

"He can't be. He's as hard as a rock."

"That's only put on for your benefit."

"Oh," I seemed to be learning things all the time.

"His parents were killed in a road crash. We're full of lame ducks here. I shall have to go soon, I can hardly stand up, I haven't eaten a thing all day."

"You can't leave me alone with Derek. He hates me . . ."

"I shall have to."

"The telephone's ringing. Can't you hear anything?" called Derek.

I rushed into the cottage. Everything was just as we left it in the morning. I snatched up the receiver. A voice said: "It's Captain Peters speaking. I just wanted to check starting times tomorrow. I have to be there at nine thirty. Have you got that? My competing time is nine fifty six, so you mustn't be late. Have you got that as well?"

"Yes," I replied scribbling the times on the pad beside the telephone.

"So you should leave no later than eight thirty. Have you got that?"

"Yes."

"Good, goodbye."

I wrote a tidy message for Tina beginning, 'Captain Peters telephoned' and putting down what he said. Then I ran upstairs to change and almost immediately the telephone rang again. This time it was Tina.

"Hello, is that Debbie?" she said. "I'm staying at the hospital. Simon is going to have X-rays; he's still unconscious, but they think he's going to be all right."

"I'm so glad," I said suddenly feeling limp with relief.

"I'll stay on tonight. Did you get back all right?"

"Yes. Somebody drove the Land Rover for me."

"Well done. I knew you would manage. I'll ring in the morning. I must go now," replied Tina ringing off.

I tore outside, shouting, "He's going to be all right. Tina's staying the night with him, just in case. But he's not dying or anything."

Derek came out of Charlatan's box. "But what about tomorrow?" he asked. "Captain Peters is taking Mainspring to the Riding Club Trials."

"I know, he telephoned. He wants his horse there at nine thirty."

"And what did you say?" asked Derek.

35

"Nothing. I just wrote it down."

"Didn't you tell him about Simon."

I shook my head. "Blithering idiot," yelled Derek. "Who do you think is going to drive the trailer? You I suppose!"

"I didn't think. Tina might have been back," I said defensively.

"Where is she? Did you get a number?" I shook my head. "I was so pleased to hear that Simon wasn't dead or anything."

Derek threw up his hands in despair. He clenched his teeth and prayed for patience.

Rosie said, "Stop being beastly, Derek; we all know you're good at it. Let's put on our thinking caps."

"Have you got one?" asked Derek rudely. "Well, you can think. I'm going to get on with the work; there's all the feeds to be mixed, Mainspring to be washed ready for tomorrow, his tack to be cleaned, the trailer to be cleaned out. And I hope one of you can plait."

"Can't we put him off?" I asked meekly.

"Put him off? Do you know how much he pays to keep Mainspring here? Ninety pounds a week—and you want to put him off! He's the best customer Simon's got. He pays for what you eat!" shouted Derek.

"Don't listen to him. He's mental. We'll think of something, never fear," said Rosie.

"I've let everyone down. I can see that now," I said. "I'm hopeless. I can't ride, or muck out quickly and I am definitely incapable of plaiting."

"I'll do that," offered Rosie. "I'm not as good as Tina

but I'll still come early and have a shot at it. You go in now and see if you can get a horse box to take Captain Peters. None of us can drive the Land Rover, that's certain."

It was evening now, a summer's evening with the midges biting, and the sun going down, and the horses banging their doors impatiently as they waited for their feeds. Breakfast waited to be washed up in the kitchen and all our beds were unmade. The terriers rushed round me pleading for their suppers while I thumbed through the yellow pages of the telephone directory looking for Horse Transporters.

I wondered what I should say to the horse box drivers. First I spoke to a Mr Tappett. I said that I was speaking for Mr Simon Ravenswood and that he needed a horse box to transport a horse to some horse trials and could he help; but Mr Tappett replied that I had left it a bit late and that he and all his mates were going to Wittington Horse Sales, and didn't I know that they were held on the first Friday of every month? I said, "thank you," and rang off. But now in desperation, Spick and Span started to yap incessantly and to run backwards and forwards to their tin dishes in the kitchen, so any more telephoning was impossible. I found a tin of dog meat in the larder and after a long time a tin opener, and gave them half each. Then Derek came in and said, "Aren't you going to help at all? Rosie's gone home," he said. "I can't do everything on my own."

"I'm trying to get a horse box," I replied. "I'll come when I'm ready."

I telephoned the livestock contractors but they

were all going to the Horse Sale like Mr Tappett and then I went outside thinking that we were in a hopeless mess and, as usual, it was my fault, because I should have told Tina about the earlier telephone call, or at least taken her number.

"No luck," I said. "We'll have to put off Peters," and now I had reached that point of exhaustion when everything seems ridiculous. "Mr Peters will have to stay away and play," I said.

"He's a Captain," replied Derek. "Have you ever ridden in a horse trial?" I shook my head giggling feebly.

"I thought so. If you had you'd know the work which goes into preparing for it—the hours of schooling."

"Well, he can't go and that's that," I said.

"But he can, because I'm taking him. I've often driven the Land Rover," said Derek.

"But you're only sixteen," I cried, sobering up. "You can't. It's against the law. Besides I bet you've never driven with the trailer hitched up."

"Yes I have. I've driven it with the jumps in the trailer."

"Well you're not driving it tomorrow," I shouted.

"I am," shouted Derek. "I care about Simon even if you don't. If we don't get there Captain Peters will take Mainspring away . . ."

"You'll crash it," I yelled. "You'll kill Mainspring and yourself."

"I can drive it," said Derek quietly. "Do you want me to show you?"

"No, I've had enough for today," I answered. "I

can't take any more, not another thing." Suddenly I didn't want to go on. I wanted some older person to appear and sort everything out. I didn't want any responsibility. I didn't want to decide anything.

"It will be your funeral," I announced. "But I shall be blamed."

We finished and I went indoors and started to tidy up. Then I made myself a sandwich and tried not to think about tomorrow. Derek appeared and heated up some baked beans and made toast for himself. We didn't speak. He walked up and down with his fists clenched and I knew he wanted to kick something, anything, to relieve his feelings.

I was too tired to speak; my head felt as heavy as lead and my shoulders ached. "Well, goodnight," said Derek at last leaving his dirty plate on the table. "Please be in the yard by five thirty."

I crawled up to my room like an animal to his lair. I didn't even undress properly, but just climbed into bed, set my clock for five o'clock and prayed, "Please God make everything all right tomorrow; make Tina come back and Simon be well, please, please ..." Then mercifully without another thought I slept.

I was in a tunnel without beginning or end and there was a great banging noise and I kept saying, "You can't get in, there's no way in."

Then I realised that the tunnel was a dream and the rest reality. Derek was banging on my door, yelling, "You've overslept. It's six thirty."

Light filtered through my curtains; birds sang.

"Get up. We've got to get Mainspring ready," shouted Derek.

"All right. I'm getting up." Suddenly I wished myself at home, at my old home, where I used to stay in bed until ten or eleven.

Derek's feet thundered away downstairs. My head felt heavy with sleep as I dragged myself from bed, drew back the curtains and saw that it was really day outside. Yesterday came back to me with a rush. I could hear one of the terriers scratching at Tina's bedroom door and the horses whinnying as Derek rushed round with feeds. Three minutes later I was downstairs. I grabbed a piece of bread off the table and ate it. Derek's dirty plate of the night before was still on the table. Spick and Span ran round and round me in circles welcoming me. Outside the stable cat waited for breakfast.

A small child greeted me in the yard. "Rosie can't come, she's ever so sorry. She was took bad in the night," he said.

"Oh no, and she was going to plait," I cried thinking aloud.

"She's ever so sorry."

"Thank you for coming."

"I've got to help the milkman now," he said and ran off, scuttling like a small animal.

"Rosie isn't coming, she's taken bad," I said.

Derek stared at me in dismay. He had a face which had suffered and had become tough I thought, looking at him. But he wasn't really looking at me, just through me.

"You'll have to plait. We'll leave the boxes till we

40

come home tonight. We can muck out with the lights on. We'll turn some of the horses out or they'll get Monday morning disease. You finish the hay-nets. Don't bother about weighing, just stuff them as full as they'll go."

We worked like maniacs without speaking. Presently the sun came out and, as we worked, sweat ran off our faces. Derek groomed Mainspring. Then he put on bandages, knee caps and a tail guard.

"Time for plaiting," he yelled, "I'll get the things from the tack room. It's eight already."

My fingers were all thumbs. The only sewing I had ever done was to make a skirt at junior school.

"I'll thread the needles," offered Derek. "We had better have six plaits and a forelock, one has to have an odd number. Damp the mane."

"Why don't you do it yourself? I'm sure stud grooms can plait," I said.

"I've never tried."

"Nor have I."

I stood on a bucket. Derek held Mainspring. The sun shone in my eyes. My shoulders ached. It took me ten minutes to do the first plait and it looked terrible. "It's all ends," complained Derek. "Space them out with the comb." It would have been funny if there had been time to think, but time was running out and Mainspring kept moving and the sun stayed in my eyes. I lost three needles in the straw, and the scissors disappeared to be found eventually under one of Mainspring's hoofs.

"It's about eight thirty and you've only done three plaits," wailed Derek, handing me a threaded needle.

At last I finished. Derek hitched up the trailer. I ran into wash. "Bring me a map for this area. It'll be by the telephone," yelled Derek.

The terriers pleaded for breakfast. "You'll have to wait," I told them brutally. "I haven't time."

The stable cat mewed pathetically. Inside, the cottage looked like the worst kind of slum. Washing my hands, I thought of poor Tina coming home to it.

It was ten to nine and Captain Peters had said that we should leave at eight thirty. I could feel panic rising inside me like a river about to break its banks. I wanted to scream. What am I doing here, I thought, slamming the back door after me. How have I got myself into this jam? Mainspring was boxed. Derek was starting the Land Rover. "Run," he shouted, "It's nine o'clock."

"He's competing at nine fifty six," I said.

"I know". We were moving now, slowly, carefully.

"Shut up. Consult the map. We have to go to Wittingley. It's beyond Andley Cross."

"Thanks a lot."

I could feel Derek's tenseness. He was as taut as a piece of wire pulled as tight as it will go. He's doing it for Simon I thought, Simon's his hero.

"Keep straight on for five miles," I said. "Till we reach Andley Cross."

"I know it that far you idiot."

"We haven't brought any lunch," I said.

"So what?"

"Or money," I added.

My stomach was rumbling.

"Can't you drive any faster?" I asked.

"Are you mad?"

The clock at Andley Cross said nine twenty.

"Turn left, then first right," I said.

Derek had a job to change gear. Cars hooted from behind.

"Keep going," I said. "There's a police car ahead."

"I wish I looked a bit older. Do I look eighteen?" asked Derek, smiling for the first time.

"No, about twelve."

"Shut up."

"It's gone."

"What?"

"The police car."

I had the map on my knees. "It's about another four miles," I said. "You're doing marvellously."

"Touch wood," shouted Derek.

"Stop, we should have turned right at the pub."

"I can't turn it," Derek said.

"Back a bit then."

He was swearing now, streams of words I had never heard before. "I can't get into reverse, you fool," he screamed. "I knew you would let me down, you stupid girl. You're worse than Rosie."

He got into reverse and we shot back and I could hear Mainspring moving about in the trailer.

"Stop," I shouted.

"I can't . . . The wheels are in the ditch."

I got out into the hot sunlight. "I'm stuck," said Derek, wiping his brow with one bare brown arm. "I've failed. We both have."

"We can still unload," I said. "There's still time. It's only three miles now. You can ride him on."

"And leave you to face the music."

"I'll be all right."

"Let's get him out anyway," said Derek.

I climbed in through the groom's compartment. The floor sloped to the left. Mainspring was dripping with sweat. "Steady, steady, it's going to be all right," I said. He had a job to stay on his feet.

Derek threw down the ramp and backed him down somehow and tacked him up.

"I'll pull up your girths," I said. "Do you want a leg up?"

"There's someone coming," said Derek in a strange hollow voice. "You'll have to take him. It's the police."

"But I can't ride well enough," I said.

He threw me up; I felt as though I was on top of the world. I shoved my feet into the stirrups.

"Don't waste any time," called Derek. "Tell the Captain that the Land Rover's broken down. Ride him gently. Keep your heels down. Don't hold on to the saddle . . ."

I rode away. Mainspring seemed to be walking on air. I rounded a corner. A long straight piece of road stretched ahead. This is a dream, I thought, rubbing my eyes. I can't be riding Mainspring. His ears were pricked in front, large comforting grey ears; one of my plaits had come undone. I bent down to pat his neck. It was hot and sticky with sweat, and he tossed his head and quickened his pace, as though saying, "We'll be late if we don't hurry."

This is it—my Waterloo, I thought, pressing him with my calves telling him to trot on. He had a marvellous stride, long and low, and there was so much in front of me—a lovely sloping shoulder, a long arched neck. I felt safe and special and rich all at the same time, and I thought this is a moment I will remember for ever.

CHAPTER FIVE

It was quite a small competition run by a riding club. A small cardboard arrow saying, TO THE TRIALS, directed me down a stony lane towards farm buildings. Mainspring began to jog. I could hear a voice calling numbers to a collecting ring. Then I heard it say "Number 37. Captain Peters, this is the last time I shall be calling you."

I pushed Mainspring with my legs and suddenly we were galloping and I was clinging on to the saddle, saying, "Steady, whoa, steady," praying that he would stop, but unable to let go of the saddle to pull on the reins. His hoofs made a great noise on the lane. I lost one stirrup and then the other. My legs went further and further back, sending him faster, without meaning to. I'm going to fall off I thought. It's just a matter of time . . . We were through a gate now. A man with a shooting stick was running towards us, shouting, "Steady there, steady." But he wasn't quick enough. Mainspring gave one triumphant buck, then I was flying through the air, hitting the ground with my shoulder, seeing stars, getting up, screaming, "Catch him, catch him. He should be in the dressage arena."

A woman caught Mainspring. Another two plaits had come undone. A tall man with a small moustache advanced towards me saying, "And who are you?" in a thin accusing voice.

"The Land Rover broke down," I stammered. "Everybody's ill."

A man with a microphone called "Captain Peters, are you ready?"

"No, my reins are broken," he said.

Somebody appeared with reins. A girl on a chestnut said, "I'll go now. I'm ready. You can have my time; not to worry."

A groom said, "Hang on, sir, I'll put a couple of rubber rings on your plaits."

I stood alone outside it all, feeling the idiot I was.

Captain Peters rode away at last.

"Come and have a cup of coffee, I've got a thermos in my Land Rover," said a tall woman with red hair. "How is Simon?"

"I don't know, but he's not dead or anything. Do you think Captain Peters is very angry? The Land Rover wouldn't go, and there was no-one else to ride Mainspring on, so I had to. It was all right till I got to the lane . . ."

"And he saw the other horses," interrupted my new found friend. "Well, you made it anyway, you had a go."

"I haven't done much riding," I cried, sipping coffee. "I'm a townie."

"You poor thing."

I handed back my cup. Derek was waving to me now.

"You made it then?" he called.

"Thank you for the coffee. It's saved my life," I said

47

before I ran to meet Derek, forgetting how rude he had been to me only a little time ago.

"The police brought me. They were quite nice considering, but of course I'm in for it," he said.

"Surely you'll only get probation," I said slowly. "I mean we couldn't manage without you. I mean you do masses of work—twice as much as Rosie."

Derek looked me up and down. "Didn't you know, that I'm on probation already? The probation officer fixed up the job with Simon."

"What did you do, anyway? Lose your temper and stick something into someone?" I asked.

"No, I'm a joy rider. I drove a car when it didn't belong to me and I crashed it."

I couldn't think of anything to say. "So you see, this time I'll be for it," he added.

"You only did it for Simon, he'll stick up for you."

"Not when Captain Peters takes Mainspring away. Did you see his dressage test just now, it was pathetic."

"I wish I was still in my home-town," I said. "Life wasn't complicated there except for the rows. It just went on day after day, breakfast, lunch, tea and dinner, school and holidays and TV, endless TV . . ."

"You weren't really living were you?" said Derek scornfully. "You were just a well-kept cabbage."

"But it was peaceful. No-one asked me to do the impossible."

"Nothing is impossible," said Derek. "Let's sit down somewhere and watch the Captain ride cross-country. Afterwards the police are finding someone to take Mainspring home—us too—They've driven the Land

Rover and trailer back to the stables themselves."

"Tina may be home," I said hopefully.

"Did you know she thinks a lot of you?" asked Derek, screwing up his eyes to stare into the sun. "She thinks you've got the makings of a rider."

"You must be mad," I replied. "Or a liar. I'm hopeless."

"She says you have a way with horses. She told me and Rosie that yesterday when we were cleaning tack. She said there are several types of rider, there's Simon who is brave and full of courage and so confident that he takes his horse with him, and then there are the ones who understand a horse's mind; the kind that can ride horses no-one else can manage. She thinks you belong to that lot."

"She didn't say that. You're inventing it," I said.

"The third type is the one who gets there by sheer hard work ... Here he comes," said Derek. "Gosh, Mainspring's puffing."

Mainspring was lathered with sweat. In spite of the rubber rings, all my plaits had come undone. "We just can't exercise them enough. Simon can't say no to anyone. Can't you talk to him? He's your brother."

"Take out what's left of those dreadful plaits before the show jumping and get him cleaned up," yelled Captain Peters over his shoulder.

We took off Mainspring's saddle and worked on him till our arms ached. And all the time I was thinking what Tina had said—that I would be able to ride horses no-one else could, and the words were like a spark of hope and joy inside which would keep me warm whatever else happened.

"We'll have to work harder to help Simon," I said.

"We can't," answered Derek. "We're all desperately over-worked, haven't you noticed. This is the third time Rosie's been ill in six months. And we never get a whole day off."

"I'll get better and I'll work faster."

"Supposing I'm sent away."

"We'll jump that fence when we come to it."

I couldn't feel despondent with Tina's words going round and round in my head. Suddenly my horizon seemed full of hope and success.

We fed Mainspring and rugged him up and wished we had money to buy something to eat. The flies swarmed round Mainspring and he broke into a sweat again. We could see Captain Peters eating sandwiches and drinking champagne with friends while our mouths watered, and our empty stomachs rumbled. "Oh to be rich," exclaimed Derek suddenly.

"We always had plenty to eat and drink in town," I said, "and smart parties, but I would rather be here."

"You've changed your tune," said Derek.

I looked around me and knew it was true. "Yes, I have," I answered.

"We had better tack up," said Derek.

I was beginning to like him. I realised that he was the sort of person who is willing to risk his neck for a friend and there are not many of them about nowadays.

We polished Mainspring with a rubber and oiled his hoofs. We wiped over his tack with a cloth and tacked him up. Then Derek led him up and down waiting for Captain Peters to finish with his friends and I sat on the grass and thought that I was happy in spite of all the disasters, happier than I had been for years, and I decided that I must be selfish to be happy when poor Simon was ill and everything had gone wrong. Captain Peters appeared at last, mounted and rode away without saying thank you.

"What a pig," said Derek, sitting on the grass beside me. "A pig without manners."

"A particularly horrible boar," I answered, beginning to laugh, "with small eyes and long tusks."

"And a bully into the bargain."

We both started to laugh. "You're better than Rosie anyway," said Derek. "She's so dumb and always sucking sweets."

"I hated you at first," I answered.

"Four faults for number 34," announced the loudspeaker.

"That's it then," said Derek, jumping to his feet.

"Look who's coming!" I yelled. "It's Tina."

She was running towards us waving. "I've brought the trailer," she yelled. "Simon's all right. He's home . . ."

"Three cheers," I yelled.

Captain Peters handed his horse to Derek. "I shall be removing him immediately," he said.

"Thank you," replied Derek. "Thank you very much."

"What happened? Why's he in such a mood?" asked Tina.

"It's a long story," I answered and suddenly my high spirits were gone, and I thought, we've let her down, and Simon, too.

51

"I've seen the police," replied Tina looking at Derek. "They said they have no choice but to take you to court. I'm so sorry. Apparently you haven't been reporting to the probation officer either."

"There just hasn't been time," replied Derek. "When I was meant to go, there was always the blacksmith, or people coming to look at horses."

"It's not his fault," I said. "We did our best today."

"I know," replied Tina. "Come on, let's box up and go home."

I felt hollow inside and faint with hunger. "I'm sorry about the cottage. There wasn't time to wash up," I said.

"And Rosie didn't come, she's ill," continued Derek. "So we couldn't muck out all the horses."

"And I overslept."

"It doesn't matter," said Tina, "let's go home."

Mainspring boxed beautifully. The rosettes were being awarded as we left. "You did your best," said Tina smiling at us. "No-one can do more than that."

Evening had come. Men were going home from work, cows were leaving milking parlours. "It's been a long day, the longest of my life I think," I said.

"We'll have something to eat, then we'll finish the work," said Tina.

Derek shut his eyes and slept.

"There's two letters for you," said Tina. "I think they're from your parents."

"Whatever have they written for," I said to stop a feeling of panic which I couldn't understand.

"They must want to know how you are."

"But why both on the same day?"

"Just coincidence, I expect."

Everything was peaceful in the evening light; the harsh colours muted; the birds twittering sleepily in hedges.

"Nearly home," said Tina.

"I'm afraid. Supposing they want me to live in London or somewhere horrible?" I said.

The horses whinnied when they saw us. Spick and Span yapped. Simon opened the cottage door and we added to the hubbub by all shouting at once—enquiries about Simon's head, his fall, and Mainspring's performance.

We unboxed Mainspring. "I've mucked out," said Rosie. "I still feel awful, but I thought I had better come after dinner. Mum says she'll come and clean up the cottage for you tomorrow, Tina. Four pounds an hour. Is that all right?"

Mainspring's box was waiting for him, his bucket full of water, a hay-net hanging in the corner, a deep bed of golden straw. We went outside.

"The Captain's been on the phone," said Simon. "He was rather abusive. He's taking Mainspring away; so we'll have to tighten our belts a bit. By the way there's two letters for you, Debbie."

He looked just the same. Tina's words came back to me and buzzed in my head. Spick and Span ran round me in mad circles licking my feet.

Simon poured us mugs of tea and handed round the biscuit tin. Tina gave me my letters. I stood staring at them afraid to open the envelopes, afraid that I was going to be hurt all over again.

CHAPTER SIX

I stood holding the letter in my bedroom. I could hear
moths fluttering against my window, and a horse
stamping in his stable. It's Cleo I thought, poor
untamed Cleo. I opened Dad's letter first. It was full
of apologies. "Penny and I are living in Oxford now.
We want you to come and see us soon; a weekend
would be best. Simon will find a train for you and we
will meet you at the station."

I remembered Penny—tall, loose limbed like a
young tree. Her few visits to our house had left Mum
in tears. She had worn smart clothes and fashionable
boots.

Mum wanted to know whether I was all right.

She had taken a lease of a flat in London which
was small but very convenient and only ten minutes
by bus from Harrods. I put the letters back in their
envelopes and went downstairs.

"Any news?" asked Simon who had been told to
rest for two days.

"Nothing special," I answered rushing outside to
help hay up for the night.

"Any news?" asked Tina.

I shook my head. "They don't want you back?" she
asked.

"No, not really. Do you want me to go then?"

"Of course not, don't be silly."

It was a lovely dreamy summer night, with the moon just rising and the sun hardly gone. Cleo welcomed me with a neigh. Derek was filling water buckets, swearing at the tap, slopping water everywhere because he was too tired to carry anything. Tina shone a torch on Charlatan's knee. "There won't be a scar," she said. "He wasn't fit, and he won't be for ages now."

"We've got too many horses," I said.

"You're dead right," agreed Tina, straightening his rugs. "We must re-organise ourselves somehow. We need your help."

We were staggering now. The moon was really up and there was a lonely bird calling and calling in the night sky. Derek hardly spoke. Spick and Span chased imaginary mice. The horses munched.

"That's the lot then," said Tina.

Rosie slipped away on her bike. I thought of Oxford, of grey colleges, of bustle and noise and the horses in Port Meadow. I imagined Mum's flat, her pretty china arranged in a glass case, her dressing table covered with pots of make-up. I felt torn apart.

"Come on, bed," said Tina.

I slept as I had never slept before. Morning came too soon, but at least today we had Tina to help, and Rosie's mother bustling round the cottage, plump and friendly in a flowered dress. And, when we went outside, Rosie was already at work, helped by a small brother who had nothing else to do. We left Simon asleep and worked steadily, but peacefully without desperation.

At ten o'clock a police officer called. He sat in the tack room talking to Derek.

"They are taking me to court," said Derek afterwards. "They say they can't do anything else, seeing that it's the second time I've taken a car."

"Why did you do it the first time?"

"I don't know, just for something to do. There was nothing in my life till I came here."

"If you're put away we're sunk," said Tina.

"They can't do it," said Rosie. "You did it for Simon."

I lunged Cleo. She pranced and danced, her tail flowing behind her like a flag, her neck arched. Tina watched from the gate. "She's your sort of mare," she said.

"She hates being cooped up. Can't she go out for a bit? Her nerves are all to pieces," I answered.

There was sweat like foam on her neck. She was looking for excitement and there wasn't any.

"All right, put her out."

She rolled and rolled and then paced round the field snorting like a mustang.

"She's mad," said Tina. "No-one will buy her."

"You could breed from her."

"No thank you. I don't want two mad ones around."

"I'll take her on," I offered.

"She'll break your neck."

"I'll risk that."

"I won't be responsible. I have to think of your parents," said Tina.

"She's under fourteen two. Derek measured her for me," I said. "I could ride her in children's classes."

56

"I'll think about it," replied Tina.

At twelve o'clock a horse box came for Mainspring. I led him up the ramp. I patted his neck and he nuzzled my pockets and I said, "We did out best, but it wasn't good enough . . ."

The driver threw up the ramp. "He'll be all right where he's going," he said. "Princes and all keep their horses there."

Tina stood small and worried. I guessed that she was thinking about the ninety pounds a week which wouldn't be coming in any more. "Don't you worry, Tina, your luck will change, just like the weather changes," said Rosie.

"He was one of my favourites," said Derek sorrowfully.

After lunch I caught Cleo. I tacked her up in a rubber snaffle, and a standing martingale. Derek legged me up and led me to the schooling paddock.

"I'm only going to walk her," I said.

"You'll fall off for certain. Then, we'll be another helper short," said Derek gloomily. "And you haven't got permission either."

I whistled to give myself courage. Cleo cocked an ear to listen. I patted her neck as we went on walking and now I didn't need to whistle any more. I rode a circle and practised stopping and starting; then I let her walk on a loose rein and she dropped her head and extended her neck and I could feel how long her stride was. Then we trotted a few strides and seemed to be dancing on air. "You are too good for me," I said but all the time a crazy plan was taking shape in my head and I was seeing myself galloping, going with

57

her, feeling the fences cleared one by one . . . "You are a winner," I told her. "Or you will be if you just calm down . . ."

I dismounted and handed Cleo oats from my pockets. Then I untacked her and putting on a headcollar took her to graze the roadside.

"You could be worth a lot," I told her. "You could be the best junior jumper in England."

She grabbed huge mouthfuls of grass. The sun was hot on our backs, and slowly the horse flies came. I swatted at them and imagined myself in Oxford walking along the Banbury Road with nothing to do . . . then Derek appeared riding Searchlight. "It's cuppa time," he said. "Yours must be stone cold by now."

"Time for evening stables, get a move on," shouted Rosie.

I had enjoyed killing the horse flies; it relieved me of some of the anger I felt mounting inside me. Anger I didn't understand, but was there nevertheless.

"So you're still alive," asked Tina. "She didn't toss you off."

"That's right, but I only walked," I said. "At heart I'm a coward."

"A wise one though. We'll let you be responsible for her if you like. But please be careful, she's a funny mare."

"I will. I promise. Thank you very much."

And now I knew why I was angry; it was because time was running out. Pressures were mounting. Soon I would have to leave, or worse still, choose— Oxford or London. My sense of peace was gone. I

58

didn't want to make a decision; I wanted to stay at Bullrock and school Cleo.

After supper we had a council of war. Simon had been doing the accounts. "We must re-organise," he said. "We are losing money. We must sell something."

"Not Cleo," I said.

He laughed. "No-one wants her. And she cost three thousand," he said. "She's a dead loss."

"I'm going to make a jumper of her," I said.

"A what?"

"A jumper," I said more quietly this time.

"For pity's sake. You must be mad," he answered. "We've had some really good people on her, and she's behaved like a maniac."

"She's changing," I answered. "I'm changing her. She's all strung up. She needs more freedom; she needs something to amuse her."

"This is the biggest joke of all," said Simon slowly. "My little sister is actually lecturing me on managing a horse—it's fantastic."

"Don't be horrible," said Tina.

"But honestly, she can't trot without holding on . . ."

"Shut up, please shut up," I said leaving the room because suddenly I was sure I was going to cry.

I heard Tina say, "You're a fool, Simon," as I shut the door behind me and ran to my room. I bumped my head on the beam and swore like Derek. I switched on my Walkman but kept hearing, "She can't trot without holding on." It isn't true. I'm getting better all the time. I know I am. But the words stayed in my brain, echoing and re-echoing, drowning the music even . . . I'm no good at anything I thought, thinking I could ride, was just a mad fantasy, and I hated Derek for repeating Tina's words about me, for giving me hope, when there wasn't any.

"Can I come in?" it was Tina.

I said, "Make yourself at home," and switched off the Walkman.

"He's cross. His head aches and we are losing money," she said. "Try and understand."

"I don't hold on any more," I answered, looking at the curtains which were patterned with prancing horses.

"I know; but he hasn't seen you riding for several days now. He doesn't know how you are coming on. You are going to be really good, better than me," said Tina.

"You don't mean it," I answered, although I felt my heart give a pleased flutter of excitement.

"What about your letters?"

"Dad wants me to stay with him and Penny."

"Perhaps you ought to go, just for a bit; he may be feeling guilty."

I started to pace the room; I felt cornered again.

"Just for a day or two. Then come back," said Tina.

"He may want me to stay."

"You will have to risk that."

"I suppose I'm a dead loss," I said.

"Idiot," exclaimed Tina. "You are cheap labour, and better labour every day. Look at yourself in the mirror, you've changed."

She left the room and I looked in the old-fashioned

gilt mirror which hung above the chest of drawers and I wasn't pale any more, my skin was sun tanned. My hair was bronzed by the sun, my eyes shone back at me. I didn't look like a weak, frightened mouse any more but strong and self-assured. I think if I hadn't been so tired I would have danced round the room then; instead I changed into my pyjamas, climbed into bed, and changed the cassette in my Walkman to Wet Wet Wet, and fell asleep with it still playing.

July had become August and suddenly a whole month had gone, but I was still afraid everything would end.

Cleo was jumping three foot now; she didn't need teaching. She simply took me over, judging everthing herself, tossing her head afterwards as though to say, "You see I can do it. I can jump anything," and deep down inside myself I knew it was true. I started to look at show schedules. To imagine impossible dreams coming true. I wrote to my parents saying that I would come later, when I had more time, when things were easier and Simon quite mended.

I rose first in the morning and rushed straight outside to Cleo who stood with her ears pricked, her nostrils nickering. I hacked her alone now through the yellowing countryside and saw that the leaves were changing colour, that the oats were being cut and I knew that it couldn't go on, that sometime someone was going to cry "Stop!" And then it would be over.

Derek was taken to a Juvenile Court. Simon went

with him, while the rest of us waited at home praying that he wouldn't be sent to a special school.

"If he goes, we will have to find someone else. We can't run the place without him," said Tina. "We only have the one room. We will have to advertise and good working pupils are not easy to find."

"He did it for Simon," I answered.

"I wish he hadn't."

"Will it be in the newspapers?"

"No. At least his name won't be mentioned," said Tina.

Later he returned with Simon. "It's all right," shouted Simon. "He's got another chance, a last chance!"

We were all suddenly happy. Rosie hugged Derek who squirmed and wriggled.

Simon said, "The old judge had a lot of sense. He believed us. He thought we looked honest. He said that everyone should have a hand to burn for a friend."

Derek went straight to work. He looked tired and embarrassed and hang-dog all at the same time.

"Jolly good," I said, carrying empty buckets to be filled.

"It was Simon. He spoke up for me. He said I was the best worker he had ever had. He said he would trust me with all his money, with anything ... I don't know why he said it, I'm not that good," said Derek with a choke in his voice.

"We couldn't manage without you. Who else could help Simon with all the young horses?" I asked.

"You. You're pretty good," said Derek.

"He thinks I'm still holding on to the saddle," I replied, beginning to laugh. "Anyway, I'm pretty hopeless compared with other people."

It was another day gone and I counted the days. I knew the end would come with the end of the summer and I didn't want to lose a single day or hour or minute . . . Simon had said "When you go, we'll have to find someone else. So please do tell us in plenty of time, won't you?"

"I'm not going till I have to," I had answered and since then every hour had become twice as precious.

So now I said to Derek, "I'm not here for ever you know. I'm under sixteen. I have to go on being educated and my parents want me back. I've got to decide whether to live in Oxford or London. Which would you choose?"

"I don't know. Oxford, I suppose, because it's easier to leave. I mean you could just walk away and in the end you would meet fields and stone walls, but London never ends," replied Derek tidying the midden.

"If I could take Cleo, I wouldn't mind so much," I said. "But I haven't any money of my own besides what Dad sent me and that's only a few pounds."

"And since you took her over she's worth more than four thousand and in another month it might be five thousand. One can't find good horses any more. They're all going abroad."

"I shall never have a horse of my own. It's too late now; in a few years' time I shall be grown up." I didn't want to grow up.

"It's all tidy now," said Derek looking round the

CHAPTER SEVEN

The rain was falling from the sky in bucketfuls. Tina, Rosie, Derek and myself were cleaning all the spare tack in the tack room. Simon had gone to Wales in search of horses to buy. I had been through all the show schedules on the tack room table.

"I want to jump Cleo on Saturday at the Stanton Show, can I? There's a Novice Class and the jumps are only two foot nine, and she jumps three foot out of a trot; it's nothing to her."

Tina picked up the schedule and looked at it.

"I shall die if I don't go. It's perfect; it's under fourteen two, under sixteen years old—everything. Please, Tina."

"I can't go with you," Tina answered. "Rosie's got the weekend off and Simon will still be away."

"I don't mind. You can tell me what to do."

"It's a very small show," Tina continued. "We don't usually go to such small ones where the prizes are in kind."

"It's an under twenty-one show," Derek said. "She can hack there. I'll go with her on my bike and come back in time to help with the evening stables. She's never been to a show before."

"I'm going out with my boyfriend," Rosie said, "Or I would offer to stay, but he's lovely, he is really. You should see his hair, it's all curly."

"I don't want you to fall off and get hurt," Tina told me. "And I don't want Cleo spoilt."

"He calls me his guardian angel, he does really. He says I bring him luck," continued Rosie.

"If she learns she can refuse three times in the ring, she will go on refusing," said Tina.

"She won't refuse."

"But she will if you go in the jump off."

"I won't. I promise."

"I'll have to square Simon."

I knew I had won, because Tina can always square Simon.

"You'll have to pay your own entries. We're broke. We can't find any more horses to buy. I don't know what's going to happen. There's another livery stable opening soon at Longmoor-under-Water and the owner is a member of the Canadian Olympic Team; so, if we can't live by dealing, we're finished."

"Why don't you open a riding school; the ponies could live out and you're a marvellous teacher, Tina," I said.

"One needs a covered school. Otherwise what do you do when it's wet?" asked Tina.

"Can't you build one?"

"They cost over ten thousand pounds and the rates are enormous."

So, they are in a jam I thought. We all are.

"I shall be leaving at Christmas," Rosie said. We hope to get married in the New Year. We are looking for a house."

"Congratulations," said Tina.

"If we can't find a house, we'll live in a caravan . . ."

I wasn't listening now. I was imagining myself on Cleo competing at my first show. I thought, I shan't sleep tonight. I shan't sleep until it's over. Later I told Cleo about it, and she nuzzled my hair and rubbed her cheek on my shoulder. And I said, "You can do it Cleo. You're the best mare in the world. You're one in a million."

Simon came back in the evening without any horses.

"They went to Germany," he said scowling. "The whole lot. There was a dealer buying for a German industrialist or someone, or perhaps it was for the government. I don't know which, but he had a heck of a lot of money . . . rolls and rolls of notes. It makes me sick, really sick . . . I stood by Bill Turpin and we bid and bid and bid. I bid three thousand and fifty for an unbroken two year old, but it still wasn't enough."

"Don't worry," said Tina. "It's always darkest before dawn. They can't go on paying these huge prices for ever . . ."

"Can't they? If they can, we're sunk," said my brother moodily, pacing up and down in the sitting room like an angry tiger.

I went to my room and thought about Saturday. I wished that my parents could be there to cheer me on, both of them standing together in old clothes looking horsy. If wishes were horses beggars would ride, I thought. One can't have everything. At least I'm going . . .

The next day I jumped Cleo round a course. Tina had wanted to watch me, but at the last minute she had to help Simon with a foal which had cut himself, so Derek put up the fences instead and stood in the centre of the course calling "Number 23, Miss Deborah Ravenswood on Cleopatra," and then he made a tinkling noise and shouted, "Don't go before the bell or you'll be eliminated."

Cleo went steadily like an old hand. I only had to go with her, keeping contact, leaning forward as she took off.

"They are only two foot six," I shouted drawing rein. "Let's put them up a bit."

"Just a few inches," said Derek. "We mustn't overface her."

"Thanks a million," I said.

"You look like an old hand too," announced Derek raising the gate. "It's extraordinary."

"I've only just started to live," I said. "I was just a cabbage before, watching other people being people on television . . ."

Cleo tossed her head. She was ready. She reached into her snaffle bit. She had the sort of canter which some horses never obtain even after years of schooling—a natural balanced canter which made her come into every fence exactly right with her hocks under her, so that there were no rough edges to her performance, stride flowed into stride, jump into jump. She made no mistake.

"If Simon saw her he'd go berserk, he'd sell her tomorrow," Derek said rushing to fill Cleo's mouth with pony nuts. "So don't tell him, Debbie. He can't keep anything good. He always sells too soon. Don't tell him anything."

"I won't. But he can't sell her, he can't . . ." I

answered, riding her back to the yard. "I couldn't live without her now. Don't you understand?"

Derek nodded. "And I can't settle in London or Oxford," I added, "and step out every morning on to a pavement either. I can't. It's impossible now."

"You had better wash her tail," said Derek.

"I shan't plait," I said. "Not ever again. I shall let her mane blow in the wind."

I thought, it won't happen, something will go wrong, I shall never make it, the stables will go on fire. I shall die in my sleep. Tomorrow is too lovely ever to come true. . .

"I've bought you some boots," said Tina when I went indoors. "Try them on." The boots were black ones made of rubber. "They're a little big but you're still growing," Tina said, feeling my toes through the boots.

"They're perfect. Thanks a million."

"Your father sent the money. I think he wanted me to buy you a dress, but I bought you these instead."

"I don't wear dresses any more," I said, walking up and down in my boots. "They feel great. I feel like an expert now. Like those professionals who keep smacking their boots with their whips and saying, 'by Jove, that mare can jump.'"

"How did she jump."

"Like a dream."

Saturday was fine. I washed Cleo's tail and mane and I body-brushed her until she glistened. Derek had borrowed Rosie's bike. We set off together, at nine forty. Cleo walking with a long eager stride, her head up, her ears pricked, Derek pedalling beside me in an old coat, a stable rubber hanging out of one pocket.

I felt very smart in my boots. I wanted to sing but I'm not very musical and I thought Derek might laugh at me.

"She's mad getting married," he said.

"Who?"

"Rosie. She's only eighteen."

I didn't want to talk. I wanted to enjoy every minute of the ride to my first show; the birds singing in the trees seemed to be singing just for me, and, when cars slowed down for us, I felt like a Princess. And Cleo's neat hoofs clip-clopping on the tarmac were like music to my ears.

"There it is," said Derek.

We could see the show now. Stewards were still putting up ring ropes while a crowd of children on ponies waited to go into the ring.

"It's going to start late," Derek said. "And we forgot to bring a headcollar."

We rode down a grassy track and into a large field full of trailers, Land Rovers and horses in tail bandages being led up and down.

"Give me a fiver and I'll enter you," Derek said.

My legs in my smart new boots felt like jelly now. I gave Derek a note. The competitors were being called into the ring for class one, jumping for ponies under thirteen two. Mine was the next class.

Cleo's head had gone up three inches higher than usual. she looked at the other horses and snorted; she started to canter sideways, to prance and dance and refuse to stand still.

"Here's your number," called Derek, "and your change."

I dismounted and tied on my number. It seemed like the greatest moment of my life for it made me a competitor, a rider—everything I wanted to be.

"Trot her round, talk to her," said Derek. He held my stirrup while I mounted, and pulled up the girths. "Relax, you're worse than she is," he added with a grin.

She trotted as though she had springs in her hoofs. I kept talking to her. I felt sick now and my heart was fluttering in a silly way.

A man in a trilby hat stared at us. He walked round behind Cleo and then in front of her. "She's not for sale," I muttered. "She's mine." But I knew it wasn't true.

The jump off had started in the ring. Cleo watched, her ears pricked, her skin quivering with excitement. Derek polished her with the stable rubber. "Oh no. Look!" he said. "There's a water jump."

Ten minutes later I was walking the course with the other competitors copying everything they did, and my heart was banging against my sides with excitement. I had never jumped water before.

There were ten jumps altogether including a combination of three jumps finishing with parallel bars.

"You mustn't lose impulsion here," said a mother to her daughter. "Push Toby on."

A father was instructing his son, "Give him a touch of the spur when you pass the collecting ring for the second time. Keep him going forward. Do you hear, son, and ride flat out at the water."

The boy was small and pale. He nodded. "Yes Dad, I'll remember."

"Hit Toby as you come into the triple," the mother said.

"Ride fast through the finish, son, and don't go before the bell."

I remounted. "Remember to wait for the bell," said Derek. "Here let me check your girths again."

"You've just checked them."

"Shall I ride flat out at the water?" I asked.

Derek nodded.

"Full speed," he said.

The man in the trilby was staring at us again. "I wish he'd go away. I hate him."

"But it's Bill Turpin," said Derek.

"Who?"

"A horse dealer. Your brother knows him."

"Number 27, you are wanted in the collecting ring," called a steward.

"Where is it?" I cried wildly.

"Over there, idiot," said Derek.

I nearly rode over some children lying in the grass. "Our first show, yours and mine. We're both in the same boat," I told Cleo.

Bill Turpin was talking to a man in a Rolls Royce. He pointed at Cleo.

"She's a late entry. I don't know either of them," he said.

"Walk her up and down. Don't let her stand with the other horses, or she'll get nappy," advised Derek.

There were three clear rounds already and the sun was still shining.

"Five more to go before you," Derek said. "Don't worry about the water and steady her a little before the combination."

"She always looks," I said.

"Touch wood," yelled Derek.

I touched the saddle, but Derek is superstitious and he rushed away and brought back a piece of dead wood and made me touch it, and then, at last, it was my turn.

I rode in slowly. I walked a circle waiting for the bell. Suddenly I felt as though I had done it all before, that this was my life and always had been. I felt Cleo relax, her ears came forward and she stopped quivering. Then the buzzer went.

It's not a bell after all I thought riding towards the first fence. Cleo took off rather late and then collected herself and cantered over the wall like an old hand. She frisked a little as she cleared the gate as though saying, "These jumps are nothing to a mare like me," and her confidence gave me confidence as we rode on towards the combination. I felt her look, judge the distance, lengthen her stride, take off, take another stride and jump; then I pushed her on and we went over the parallel bars. And now I was riding flat out towards the water jump. I shut my eyes as she took off. I felt her stretch, and then we were over. I heard a quick burst of clapping as I turned for the oxer, the Sussex gate, the triple. I remembered to ride through the finish. It was my first competition and we had jumped clear. I slid to the ground. Derek stuffed Cleo's mouth with oats. I showered her neat grey neck with pats. "We did it," I cried. "All of it, even the water."

"If only Tina had been here," Derek said.

"Or my parents," I added. "They've never seen me succeed at anything."

"You're in the jump off."

"I know."

The sun shone hot on my back. We watched the stewards put up the jumps. I forgot my promise to Tina as I mounted, and Derek checked my girths once again.

Cleo entered the ring for the second time like an old hand. She tossed her elegant head and glanced at the crowd on the other side of the ring ropes. She dropped her nose and danced a little. I heard someone say, "I like that grey," before the buzzer went and Derek called, "Good luck."

We went round again, steadily, carefully, like experts. Bill Turpin was waiting for us as we came out.

"I want to buy your mare," he said.

"You can't," I answered without hesitating. "She isn't for sale."

"Not for five thousand pounds?"

"Not for anything."

We jumped once more against the clock. I was the last to go, which gave me an advantage. Two of the earlier competitors had knocked fences. A boy on a piebald had jumped a slow, careful, clear round and a girl on a chestnut had done the course in forty-seven seconds with one foot in the water.

Derek checked my girths once again. I rode in slowly. "Don't hurry, just cut the corners a bit and you'll be all right," said Derek.

"Good luck," said a little girl I had never seen before.

We didn't touch anything. We jumped the course in fifty seconds and I rode back in first, with Cleo striding out, looking every inch a winner. A steward told me where to stand. A lady in a flowered hat gave me a red rosette and a cup.

Without thinking I said, "I thought the prizes were in kind. I didn't expect a cup."

"We always give a cup for the Novice jumping," answered the steward.

The lady patted Cleo. "We expect to see you at Wembley next year," she told me. "Well done."

I cantered round the ring with the rosette between my teeth and the cup in my left hand. I could feel tears of joy pricking behind my eyes while the spectators clapped.

Bill Turpin was waiting for me again. "Six thousand. Come along, dear, you'll be too old for her next year. She'll be wasted on you then."

"She's not for sale," I replied, my face in Cleo's mane, trying to forget that she wasn't mine.

"She's lovely," said the little girl who had ginger hair and freckles. "Have you had her long?"

I shook my head. Derek loosened the girths. "We can go home now. She's done more than enough for her first time out. Let's give her a drink," he said.

We led her across to a water trough. "I wish she was mine," I said.

"We all wish for things we can't have. You've got a cup. No-one can take that away from you, or the glory," replied Derek.

"I would swap a hundred cups for Cleo," I answered.

As I started for home, I remembered my promise to Tina. I had broken it. I had jumped a second and a third round. Would she mind? Would she ever trust me again?

At the roadside people were eating picnic lunches. Far away a clock struck one. "It was the greatest moment of my life," I said.

"Not many people win a cup their first time out," Derek agreed.

"Bill Turpin offered six thousand pounds for her."

"What?"

"Six thousand."

"What did you say?"

"That she wasn't for sale."

"You had better keep quiet about it then," said Derek grimly.

"I know I'm selfish," I answered, "and a liar."

"She isn't yours. You haven't the right to answer."

I tried to whistle but suddenly I couldn't.

"She's the only thing that matters," I announced after a time. "Can you understand?"

"She isn't yours. . . Don't spoil everything."

"Lots of people win on horses which don't belong to them. I'm just trying to make you face facts. It will be easier in the long run. Just stop kidding yourself. Grow up."

The sky was an endless sea of blue. The fields were yellow where the corn was already ripening.

"I'm going on ahead. You'll be all right now," said Derek.

"You won't tell them."

"What?"

"Anything."

"All right."

I started to sing a long sad song as Derek rode away.

The road was empty, the fields were empty. There was just me and Cleo and the road home. I looked at the cup. Soon it would have my name on it. I had ridden a winner my first time out. The jumps had been too small for a mare like Cleo. She was going to be a champion.

I could see the stables in the distance now. Lunch time was over. Tractors started up in the fields, men came out of pubs wiping their mouths on their sleeves. A mother with two small children ran for a bus. It was just another day, an ordinary day for nearly everyone, but for me it was a turning point, a day I would never forget.

CHAPTER EIGHT

The yard was full of the peace of a late summer afternoon. Everything was swept up tidily, the brooms standing upside down, wheelbarrows put away and the horses leaning over their loose-box doors dreaming of who knows what.

Derek and Rosie were cleaning tack. I could hear the hoover going in the cottage. I had dismounted and started to untack when Tina came out. She looked at Cleo's bridle. She stared at me.

"A rosette and a cup! You won!" she cried. "Well done."

The shadow of Bill Turpin still hung over me. "Yes, we won. I jumped off. I forgot my promise. I'm sorry, terribly sorry."

"But you succeeded. Don't do it again, though." She patted Cleo. "A cup your first time out. How many times did you jump- off?"

I told her everything except about Bill Turpin.

"Must we tell Simon about my win?" I finished. "If he knows, he'll sell Cleo won't he?"

"But she does belong to him, and he'll be so pleased," Tina answered.

"It was only a little show. The jumps were tiny. She took me round," I said. "I didn't do anything. She didn't even stop at the water."

"Water! Was there really a water jump?"

I nodded. "Don't let Simon sell her please, Tina. I'll save up. I'll get Mum and Dad to subscribe. I'll sell my Walkman, everything I've got."

I couldn't look at Tina now; instead I looked away across the paddocks to where elms stood, ancient and still in the distance. I was trying not to cry. Cleo wanted to come in again now because of the flies. She whinnied to me and pawed the ground.

"She wasn't any good before," I said. "He couldn't sell her. I'll buy her. I'll raise the money somehow. I'll borrow it. I'll write to all my relations." I slipped a rope round Cleo's neck and led her back to her box.

"She's worth a lot now, probably five thousand at least," replied Tina, shutting the loose-box door. "But we'll see what Simon says when he comes back."

"Thank you."

"Well done," cried Rosie hugging me. "I always knew you were going to be a winner."

"It was Cleo," I said.

Simon came back late. I could hear Tina talking to him downstairs. I sat in my room playing my tapes.

In the morning Tina said, "You're going to see your father today. It's all fixed up. He rang last night after you were in bed." And for an awful moment I thought, it's a plot. They're going to sell Cleo while I'm away. They know about Bill Turpin.

"Why today? Why not tomorrow? Why do I have to go."

"Why are you so excited and upset? It's perfectly normal for your father to want to see you," reasoned Tina.

"But why today?"

"Perhaps he has a day off work. It's Sunday after all. Pack some pyjamas and a tooth brush. You're catching the nine fifty five train. Cleo's resting after the show."

"Is anyone coming to look at horses?"

"Not as far as I know."

The train was almost empty. I sat staring out of the window imagining myself galloping across the landscape on Cleo.

Dad met me at Oxford. He hadn't changed. Taking my case he said " We'll catch a bus. I hear you've become a rider."

I wanted to say then, "Please, can you lend me some money? It's important, terribly important." But I thought, it's too early. Hold your horses, Debbie. Wait till after lunch. So I simply nodded.

"Are you happy with Simon and Tina?" he asked. I nodded again. I didn't want to talk about it. I didn't want my life at the stables mixed up with Oxford and the endless traffic and the fumes. It was too precious.

"We have to think about school," Dad said.

"Term begins in three weeks and you aren't down for any school. It's a terrible situation."

"Yes," I said.

"Do you know what you want to do when you're grown up?" asked Dad as we boarded a bus.

"Ride horses."

Dad shuddered slightly. "Are you sure?" he asked.

"Yes absolutely. I want to break and make them," I answered firmly sitting down.

"I thought you might like to live here with me in

term time. There are several first class schools and Penny's left."

I didn't know what to say. "I'm so sorry," I muttered and then, "What a beast!"

"It's so beautiful here, don't you think so, Debbie?" he asked.

"If you like a town, yes."

"You wouldn't like to go to college here?"

"No, thank you. I want to be a show jumper," I answered. "I want to go to Wembley and Hickstead. I want to jump for England." And instead of the traffic, I heard a great crowd clapping; I felt a horse's stride beneath me, jumping, clearing fence after fence. "I'm addicted," I said. "It's like a drug, and I'm incurable."

"We get off here," Dad said.

The leaves were falling off some of the trees already.

"Here we are," said Dad taking my arm. "I've got an apartment."

We went inside, and upstairs into a dim dark brown room lined with books. "It's my study. Do you like it?"

"Yes."

"It's rather masculine, I'm afraid."

There were two bedrooms, a kitchen and a bathroom.

The sitting room looked on to a sad town garden.

I missed the smell of horses.

"Sit down. Would you like a pineapple juice or something?"

He fetched me a Coke and lit the oven in the kitchen.

"You can't stay with Tina and Simon forever," he

said handing me a glass. "It isn't fair on them."

"They say I'm a help. If they employed a groom they would have to pay him. I'm free, sweated labour," I answered.

I felt as though I was fighting for my life. "They say they like having me," I added in a small frightened voice. "They do really."

I thought I would wither, shrivel up and die if I had to live here now. What would I do all day? On Saturdays and Sundays? In the evenings?

"We could go to theatres and cinemas, and there's horses on Port Meadow. They look as though they need looking after," Dad said.

"But they're not Cleo," I answered.

"Who is Cleo?"

"My mare, well, sort of. She could be," I answered, my voice trailing away.

"Have they given you Cleo?"

"No. She's worth at least four thousand pounds. I want to buy her. I must," I said. "Will you help me?"

Dad looked at me. "I don't know," he answered. "Everything's such a muddle. We must get school sorted out first. It's vital."

"Please, Dad, please . . ."

"I'll think about it," he said. "But I'm not a rich man, you must know that."

We ate roast chicken and vegetables, ice cream and cheese for lunch. Then we walked down to Port Meadow where horses and cows roamed amid a profusion of ragwort; trains rushed by; and the river was sparkling blue in the sunlight.

"You could walk here as much as you liked. You

could get a Saturday job at a riding school," Dad said.
"But first of all we must settle on a school. There's a
private one on the Banbury Road. I've made inquir-
ies. I've even seen the headmistress. They can take
you. It's quite a small school. I think you could be
happy there."

"I want to go to a state school," I answered. "If you
don't mind. I would like any money you have over for
Cleo." I could sense my father's exasperation. "Anyway, I want to discuss everything with Mum as well
before I decide anything finally," I finished.

"We can be put in prison if you don't go to school."

"Yes, I know." I was playing for time. "I must see
Mum too." We had tea in a teashop full of undergrad-
uates and old ladies in hats eating alone; then we
walked past Magdalen College and fed some deer in
a park. The bells were ringing for evensong now and
everything looked beautiful in the evening light but
not as beautiful as the long tree-elmed roads near
Bullrock, nothing could beat them. And I compared
the munch of horses to the bells, and the rows of
beautiful heads to the majestic colleges, and the
horses won every time.

I slept in the spare room and dreamed that a girl in
a red macintosh was riding Cleo. She jumped her
over the yard gate and rode her over the cross-
country course. She was small and light with yellow
hair. Her father was an American and they said,
"We'll have her, Mr Ravenswood. Just name the
price."

I shouted, "No you can't, she's mine." Simon slapped
my face and the slap woke me up and I found that I

83

was crying and that dawn had come with a chorus of bird song.

I waited until seven o'clock before I made some tea and took it into Dad on a tray. I sat on his bed and said, "Listen Dad, I must have four thousand pounds. It's very important. I want a cheque at once. I can't wait."

"I haven't got it but we'll talk about it when you're at school, when your education is settled. That must come first," he said.

I put my head in my hands. "I've got to go to work today. Shall I put you on a train for Bullrock?" asked Dad, rather wearily. "See your mother as soon as you can. I'll write. We must get everthing sorted out."

"You could go back, couldn't you?" I asked slowly. "You're not divorced yet. You could live together again—buy a house."

"I must get up now," he said. "Go and dress. And put some water on for eggs. Hurry."

We didn't talk much at breakfast. There didn't seem much to say. The sun was shining outside and I was terrified that I would find Cleo gone when I returned to the stables. Because of this, I had difficulty in eating anything.

Dad kissed me goodbye at the station. "Think about school. Come again soon. And here's some pocket money," he said, handing me a ten pound note.

"Thank you very much. I'm sorry to be going," I said slowly. "I would like to live here, if there were fields and horses, really, I promise . . . It's just that I hate towns now, you do understand, don't you? I like being with you."

84

"Yes, I understand. I quite understand, but we must decide about school. Time is running out, and education is important."

"Yes." My train was waiting. I ran towards it without looking back.

The train journey seemed endless. The train stopped at every little station. People got on and off, children, mothers with huge shopping bags, men in suits.

I fell asleep and the rumble of the train became hoof beats and I was galloping across sands into a sea. The water grew deeper and deeper and the waves dragged me down. I tried to hold on to Cleo's reins, to hold her up but she sank before I did. I opened my eyes and we were in the station three miles from Bullrock. I seized my small case. There was no-one waiting on the platform. Outside the station was a small country road, lined with green verges, bedecked with meadowsweet. I started to run. God make her be there, I thought.

It was lunch time. A road worker sat eating his sandwiches on the verge while a solitary plane droned overhead. Under a clump of trees a group of horses stood head to tail. Quite soon I could see the elms which stood along the ridge beyond Bullrock. I ran faster forcing my legs to go on running until I reached the familiar stretch of road with grey walls on each side. I could see the stables now and Cleo was still there dozing, her head hanging over her loose-box, her lower lip drooping. She raised her head and whinnied.

"I'm back, and you're still here," I yelled.

Simon and Tina were having lunch. "We've kept some for you. Why didn't you ring up from the station," Tina asked.

"I didn't want to bother you," I answered, throwing down my case.

"Well, how was Dad?" Simon wanted to know.

"He wanted me to stay, to go to school in Oxford, but I can't bear it. I want to stay here. Do you mind?"

I had meant to talk about it sensibly, but now everything came out in a rush. "I'll work for my living. I don't want to be paid," I added. "I can do my share of the work before and after school. I'm getting quicker all the time."

"You want to go to the local school?" asked Tina.

"Yes. I can catch the school bus every morning."

"We had better ring up the headmaster," Simon suggested.

"I want to leave school as soon as I can. I want to make a career with horses. If you're tired of me, I'll find a job somewhere else as soon as I'm old enough." I was trying not to plead. I wanted to be independent and not a burden.

"That's all right," replied Simon taking his dirty plate to the sink. "I want to see you ride after lunch. I'll give my answer then. Be in the jumping paddock at two o'clock on Cleo."

"Of course you can stay, as long as you like, for ever," said Tina, squeezing my arm. "We love having you."

"You don't mean it. You're just being nice."

"I do," said Tina. "You're an asset, a profitable proposition."

I helped with the washing up, then I changed into jodhpurs and tacked up Cleo. Rosie has just returned from lunch. "So you're back?" she said. "Did you have a good time? Did you go to the pictures?"

I shook my head. We walked and talked, and settled nothing. I swung into the saddle.

"Didn't you want to stay home with your Dad then?" she asked.

"It isn't home. I haven't got a home. I would like this to be my home, but it isn't, worse luck," I answered, riding towards the paddock.

"There's your Mum's place, isn't there?" she insisted.

"It's in London," I answered, as though that was an answer in itself.

CHAPTER NINE

I thought, sit up, heels down, Debbie. This is your big chance. Your last hope. Flies buzzed round Cleo's head. Simon appeared and started to put up jumps. "We'll start with a two- foot-six course—all right?" he asked.

"Yes."

"Well, warm her up, jump the cavaletti," he said.

I rode her round and round. I changed rein and jumped her over the grid which was up. I felt quite brave. I thought if she knocks everything down it won't matter, because he won't want to sell her then.

"Ready?" shouted Simon.

"Yes."

Cleo jumped round steadily without hesitation. Simon put the fences up.

"Go round again," he said grimly, without smiling. I thought, I'll made her jump badly this time. I'll pull her up . . .

"What do you think you're doing, you fool," he cried as I turned her away from the first fence at the last minute.

"Nothing. I can't make her go over. It's too high," I shouted.

"I'll get on her in a minute," yelled Simon. "Ride properly, do you hear?"

"It's too high, she can only jump two-foot-six."

"Ride her properly or else go," shouted Simon. "I'm not having her spoilt. She's a born jumper."

"I'm not spoiling her; it's too high," I said slowly, calmly. "I know."

"It isn't. I'll get Derek. He's lighter than I am. He can jump her. And if you won't do what you're told, you can't stay. Is that clear?" Simon bellowed.

I knew he had won. I turned Cleo towards the first jump and used my legs. The course was higher than I had ever jumped before. Half way round I lost a stirrup, and twice I flopped on Cleo's neck, but it didn't deter her.

"What did I say? She's a champion," yelled my brother. "You've made her a champion, Debbie!"

"She's worth thousands and thousands." And now without warning I felt cold; my teeth started to chatter.

"We must take her to a show—there's one next week. The entries may not be closed. It's a big affair with an under sixteen novice jumping. You can jump her, Debbie. We'll get you a black jacket."

I couldn't speak.

"I know dozens of people who would buy her to-morrow, if they could see her jump, she's a natural, Debbie," continued my brother. "And so are you. You've improved beyond words, you're terrific. And she's still Grade C—a novice."

"Yes, I know," I said dismounting.

"We'll get her measured tomorrow and registered. This is the best thing that's happened in months," cried my brother running towards the house, calling, "Tina, Cleo can jump. She's going to be a champion."

I took Cleo back to her box and rubbed her down. She nuzzled my hair and breathed down my neck, while outside Spick and Span chased each other yapping across the yard.

"You're worth thousands, Cleo, thousands, and I'm going to have a black jacket," I said.

I found Simon on the telephone. "Yes. Are all the entries closed? Not yet. Oh good, terrific. I want to enter my sister . . ."

"Have a cuppa," said Tina. "And well done."

"That's settled," said Simon putting down the telephone. "Where's an envelope. I want to catch the next post. We'll have to get Debbie a black jacket."

"I've got ten pounds," I answered.

"You'll need a hair-net and gloves. You must look the part."

"I've got a black jacket upstairs which may fit," said Tina. "And she can tie her hair back, she doesn't need a hair-net."

"I'll just take this to the post," said Simon licking an envelope. "I want Cleo's shoes checked and her mane and tail pulled, and we had better find her a decent rug, and bandages, the lot. She's got to look expensive."

"Let's try on the jacket first," said Tina.

The arms were a little long. "I'll take them up. It's quite easy. Wait a minute while I get some pins," Tina said.

Suddenly I wanted everything to be a dream. I wanted to go back to the first day when I had just arrived, to live through it all again, and then never arrive at this moment.

"Supposing I fall off?" I asked Tina. "Simon will be furious. Is it a very big show?"

"Well, it's not exactly small," replied Tina, her mouth full of pins.

"The first prize is five hundred pounds."

"But we are not going for that are we?" I asked.

"Well, there is the glory," said Tina.

"And Cleo," I added. "It will send up her value . . ."

"We are in business, Debbie," said Tina. "We've been losing money for a long time. You can't blame Simon if he wants to make some . . ."

"I just wish it wasn't Cleo. Why couldn't it be Charlatan, or one of the others?" I asked. "I've never had a horse to myself before."

Later Simon told me that I was going to London the next day.

"Mother wants to see you," he said. "Cleo can be turned out for a bit. You will have to pay your own fare though, there isn't any money in the house until one of us goes to the bank."

"That's all right, I've got some," I answered, and I thought that it would be nice to get away from the mounting pressures for a day, to forget the approaching show and what might happen there and afterwards.

So the next morning found me at the station again boarding a train full of business men, clutching a bunch of flowers which I had gathered for Mum. This time I didn't dream ride Cleo across the passing landscape. Instead I sat imagining life without her. I saw myself going to school, studying for my exams again. What would I take? Did it matter? Did anything matter in life any more at this moment? I wished that something was settled, that I could say, this is my home, I live here . . . I was beginning to feel like a parcel again.

Mum was waiting at the barrier; I gave up my ticket then we were hugging each other and she was saying, "But you've changed, darling, you've grown or something," standing back to look at me properly in my shirt and trousers and desert boots. "You're brown, and you look so well, and Tina says you can ride, that you're going to be a champion one of these days," she cried.

We went outside into the breathless air of London in the summer.

"We can catch a bus. Tell me everything," Mum said.

"I don't know where to begin" I answered. "There's so much to tell. I made an awful muck of things in the beginning. I was useless . . ." and suddenly arriving at Bullrock, Simon's accident and Captain Peter's anger all seemed to belong to another life.

"Tell me about you. Where do you live?" I said. "Are you all right?"

We caught a bus. "Look! Look over there . . ."

"At what?" said Mum.

"At the horse, look there's a policeman on a horse," I cried. He was grey like Cleo, but heavier with a Roman nose.

"What about school?" asked Mum, unlocking the door of the flat.

92

"There's a local school. I can catch a bus. And you won't have to pay a thing, not even the bus fare."

"You want to stay with Simon and Tina then?"

"It's not just with them, it's the horses, everything. I want to be a show jumper," I replied looking round my mother's elegant flat where the satin cushions wore tassels and the curtains were thick and reached to the ground.

"I don't belong here," I said.

Mum looked worried. "I don't want to be beastly, darling," she said after some time. "But are you sure they want you? I can't believe that you are a great deal of help after such a short time."

"I can ride now," I replied. "I'm much better than Rosie."

"I can see we'll have to have a family meeting," said Mum. "We won't settle anything any other way, but you know darling, I have got a spare bedroom, and it can be yours for ever if you like. Come and see."

It looked out on to a square where a cat sat sunning himself. The houses opposite were all the same. There was a bed with a shiny cover on it, and a white dressing table and a fitted cupboard with louvred doors—that was all . . . It wasn't a big room, but long and narrow with wall-paper the colour of sand.

"Thank you," I said politely. "It's a nice room."

"You could buy yourself a picture or two to brighten it up, and you could choose some more exciting curtains."

"Yes," I replied with my heart aching for my little room at Bullrock with the birds singing in the tan-

93

gled branches of the trees outside my window, the dogs scratching at the door and the crazy beam down the middle.

"It's a very nice room Mum, but . . ."

"But what?"

"It isn't me." I sank into one of the sofas. "What would I do all day Mum?" I asked.

"There are exhibitions, theatres, museums, the International Horse Show. There's plenty going on."

It was like being offered bread after one has tasted chocolate.

"Thank you very much," I said. "I love you Mum and Dad; I do really, but I can't live without horses now. It just isn't possible."

I started pacing the room. I thought, the stable yard will be quiet now. Simon will be doing the accounts. Tina will be washing up. Rosie and Derek will be cleaning tack, or watering the horses down in the bottom paddock. The air will smell of flowers, of stables and horses, and of the sugar beet soaking in the feed shed. And the clip clop of hoofs coming along the road, the creak of saddles and the jingle of bits will sound better than any symphony.

I started to tell Mum about Cleo, about the four thousand pounds which might buy her, if I was quick enough, if only I could find it before Saturday.

We ate lunch together near the window and we could hear London going on outside, and it was lovely to be with Mum again. We talked about clothes and whether I had any boyfriends and whether Tina and Simon would ever make any money. And then later we went for a walk in a park. When a crowd of horses went by I thought, What am I doing here? I don't belong. I belong with the horses.

After that we drank tea in the kitchen and Mum asked me about my next show and promised to help me find four thousand pounds somehow. Then it was time to go, and I was wishing that life could be different, that we could all be together at Bullrock, Mum, Dad and myself.

"Ring me up after the show," said Mum taking my arm, "I'll be thinking about you all day."

"Don't you get lonely?" I asked.

Mum shook her head. "I've got plenty of friends," she said.

I bought a magazine about horses to read on the train. "Come again soon," Mum said. "Or perhaps I will come down and see you and Simon."

"Yes, that will be super, you can see Cleo then. She really is fabulous."

I sat beside a large woman with two small children. She kept handing them sweets and I could see that they would have black teeth quite soon by the way they devoured them. Mum kissed me through the open window and I decided that I was sick of saying goodbyes. Then the train pulled away and I opened the magazine and tried to forget Mum's face at the window and the fact that we were separated and would always be separated.

Gradually we left the houses behind, the gas works and the rubbish dumps, the smell of petrol fumes, and the factories. We passed rough fields where ponies were tethered, and country roads with small cottages and stately homes looking unreal in smooth fields. We came to grey walls and stone houses, and a river winding between willow trees, and then I was back at Bullrock.

Simon was waiting for me at the station in the Land Rover with Spick and Span who jumped higher and higher trying to lick my face.

"How was she?" he asked, opening the passenger door.

"All right," I said.

"You can stay if you want to," Simon said. "You've proved yourself. I never knew you could really ride."

"Thank you."

"You can be a working pupil," he continued, "but we can't pay you anything, you'll have to work for your keep. I'm sending two horses to the Horse Sale at Reading this week, two of the young ones. It's a pity but there it is."

The evenings were drawing in. It was dusk already with an autumn mist coming down over the fields.

"We need to expand," my brother continued, "and we can't. When Rosie goes we won't be able to employ anyone to replace her. I haven't done well with the young horses this year."

We were back now. The horses in the loose-boxes were munching at hay-nets.

"You had better hack Cleo tomorrow, and the next day we'll do some more jumping. I'll put up a new course, something a bit more tricky with a water jump," said Simon getting out of the Land Rover. "Mother was all right, wasn't she?" he added. "I mean she looked all right?"

"Yes. She says she's got lots of friends," I said.

96

"That's all right then." His shoulders were bent as he walked into the cottage. Suddenly he seemed older, burdened down by worries. I started to wonder how much I cost to feed, to feel guilty.

Derek was in his room reading HORSE AND HOUND. "You came back then," he said. "I can't think why. Didn't you like the bright lights?"

"Of course not. I couldn't live in a town, you know that. Could you?"

"Not unless I had lots of money and could ride in Hyde Park every day. Charlatan's lame again. Did you know? We've had the vet. He's got to be turned out, and he may have to be fired and he's only a young horse. That's why Simon's so gloomy. All our hopes are pinned on you now . . ."

"On me? You must be mad."

"On you, chum."

I looked round Derek's room. His clothes lay on the floor, his bed was unmade.

"I shall have to leave soon anyway," he said. "I can't be a working pupil for ever. I want a wage, a nice fat wage . . ."

"Oh shut up," I cried. "You can't leave now, when everything's wrong."

"It all began with Captain Peters taking away Mainspring, then the old girl moved Heather down to the new stables, and Charlatan hurt himself; and none of the young horses are ready to compete yet because they are all too young," Derek said.

"How old are they?"

"Three and four year olds. Some of them will be perfect next year. But you can't sell a four year old

97

for a great sum of money, because he isn't ready to do a lot of competing, he might get splints and spavins. And if they don't pay the telephone bill, that will be cut off next," continued Derek in the same gloomy voice.

"How do you know?"

"I saw the final demand on the door mat, and the vet bills have been enormous lately."

"We need to expand. I think you're being absolutely beastly," I shouted.

"Then there's the foals; they need lots of vitamins; and you can't sell foals, so they are just another liability. The three horses at livery are being kept too cheaply because oats have gone up by five pounds a hundredweight."

"Everything will be all right in time. Simon is going through a bad patch. We all have bad patches in our lives. He needed a big win and he didn't get it. Once he starts winning, everyone will be sending their horses to be schooled at a hundred pounds a week each. And stop looking at SITUATIONS VACANT," I shouted looking over his shoulder. "You're not leaving yet, not till we find a new working pupil. Simon stood up for you in Court the other day, so now you can stick by him."

"I'm not looking yet. I'm just considering future possibilities," replied Derek.

"Supper," yelled Tina. "Hurry up or it will be cold."

She sounded worried and on edge. Supper was a strangely silent meal and I kept recalling Derek's remark . . ."All our hopes are pinned on you now," and wondering exactly what he really meant.

Spick and Span were subdued and as soon as supper was over Simon said, "I'm going to the pub," and vanished.

"Are you looking forward to Saturday?" Tina asked me, carrying plates to the sink. "It's a very grand show."

"I'm not experienced," I answered. "I'm not good enough Tina. Supposing I fail. Supposing I let Simon down?" I asked and I knew now that I wouldn't rest until Saturday was over.

"Don't worry. It doesn't really matter," replied Tina. The result won't alter the fate of nations." But looking at her face I knew it did matter. In some peculiar unexplained way, Cleo and I stood between The Bullrock Stables and disaster. We were the last hope, the last chance. If we failed everyone would lose faith in the stables, including Derek.

I don't want so much responsibility, I thought, helping Tina with the washing up. And I wished that I was going to the little show again with Derek on an old bike, just for fun, instead of to a big posh show with all the honour of the stable on my shoulders.

CHAPTER TEN

The pressure was on now, there was no escaping it. Simon schooled me over jumps, building them higher and higher, yelling, "Keep contact. Don't throw your reins away you idiot. Keep her balanced. Steady. Don't rush."

He yelled and raved and praised and apologised. Now I knew how much was at stake, I couldn't sleep any more. I started to count the hours, to wake up in the night sweating with trepidation, to dream that I was falling, turning over and over in the air, while a crowd roared their disapproval. Tina started to feed me a special diet, to say things, like "You must keep your strength up for Saturday," to cook me eggs for breakfast and to hand me glasses of milk at odd hours.

Cleo was given the Bullrock treatment. Her mane and tail were pulled, her fetlocks trimmed, her shoes were removed and put on again. She was given a smarter rug, tail bandages. A forward cut jumping saddle replaced the old one I had been using and a newer, posher snaffle bridle was adjusted to fit her beautiful head. I was provided with a riding whip, gloves because it might be wet, and then my reins would be slippery. And all the while time was passing, inescapably. Cleo's oats were increased. On

Thursday I had my last practice before the Show. I was so nervous that I fell off into the triple and my nose wouldn't stop bleeding while Simon paced up and down the paddock, saying, "Oh no, not today of all days!" Tina fetched me a cold wet sponge and Rosie said, "Lie back, Debbie."

"She will have broken the mare's nerve, or her own," cried my brother furiously.

"If I lie back I'll be sick," I replied thinking that my brother looked like an angry toddler who had mislaid something.

"We must produce something worthwhile," Simon cried staring at me. "Can't you understand. We need success, Debbie. Nothing succeeds like success."

I stood up at last. I wasn't afraid. I was as desperate as Simon now. We need success, I thought. Our life depends on it. Cleo sensed my desperation and jumped faultlessly. The very air seemed to relax, as though we had all been charged with electricity like the sky before thunder, and now the electricity had gone. Simon gave Cleo a handful of horse nuts. "I'm sorry, Debbie," he said. "I know I'm horrid at times."

"It doesn't matter," I said. "It makes me ride better."

I felt exhausted. Derek took Cleo from me. "Go and have some tea. You need it," he said.

"Don't let Simon get you down. You can't save all this in one afternoon," Tina told me, pointing at the terriers playing, at the horses' heads hanging over loose-box doors, at everything we both loved so much. "He hasn't any business sense and nor have I, and some people don't pay their bills. The dear Captain

101

hasn't paid his yet and it's over four hundred pounds. He's trying to sue us for negligence. Of course it won't stick, but in the meantime, we have to pay a solicitor to answer his letters and he keeps his money."

"Negligence?" I cried. "What does that mean?"

"Not looking after his horse properly."

"That's a lie!" I cried.

"Exactly. It is, but we still have to prove it."

"This is just a bad patch, Tina," I said. "It will pass."

"I hope so. We are so lucky having all this. I don't want to lose it and neither of us is qualified to do anything else. That's why I want you to study, Debbie," Tina said, her dark eyes searching my face. "I don't want you to struggle like we struggle . . ."

"I like struggling," I replied, staring round the yard my eyes suddenly full of tears. "I wouldn't change this yard for all the offices in the world."

"You could work in a hotel, in publishing, there's so many things you can do with qualifications," sighed Tina. "And you could have plenty of money and no worries."

"I'm happy here," I said. "And that is what matters."

We drank tea together in the kitchen and afterwards I helped Tina back one of the young horses. By then it was time for evening stables and another day had gone. Now there was only one left between me and the Show.

"Take Cleo out for a quiet hack tomorrow," Simon said at supper. "About an hour will do, as early as you can. Okay?"

"Okay," I answered.

"It's the first Friday in the month so I'll be going to the sale in Reading," Simon said. "Not to buy of course, but to see how much ours fetch. I'll have to load up at eight and, being young horses, they may be difficult."

"I'll be about," Tina replied. "but I hate them going."

"It can't be helped," said Simon leaving the table abruptly.

The next day it rained. I rode across damp fields, through dripping woods, and told Cleo all about tomorrow and how all our hopes depended on her. I had watched the two young horses, a dark brown gelding called Moonraker, and a light chestnut mare called Mimosa, loaded into the trailer, and had looked away when I saw that Tina was crying. I felt melancholy. Rosie was leaving soon to get married and Derek was still dreaming of more profitable jobs, and I had to finally settle where I was going to school. I thought, if we all leave, Tina and Simon will have no help at all. It will be the end of everything. And I remembered how they had taken me in, fed me, clothed me, taught me to ride, and I thought, they are too generous, they don't charge enough. They should have charged Mum and Dad for my keep.

"I've telephoned the school in Belham," Tina told me at lunch. "School starts in ten days. The headmaster wants to see you. Personally, I think it would be better if you went to school in Oxford. You could still come her for weekends. . ."

"Okay, okay." I didn't want to talk about school now. I wanted to leave everything until after tomorrow. If I failed, I would leave quietly like a beaten dog. I would go to London or Oxford and forget about horses and become a secretary. Everything was settled in my mind now. It all depended on tomorrow.

Tina made me sit down all afternoon. "You must keep up your strength," she said. "Derek is doing your tack. Rosie is washing Cleo. I'll see that your clothes are all right."

"But . . ." I began.

"No buts."

It all depends on me, I thought looking round the cottage, thinking, Debbie relax.

In the evening Dad telephoned.

"We must get something settled Debbie," he said, "One way or the other, term starts in ten days."

"I know," I answered.

"Well then, you have to go to school, it's the law of the land."

"It's all right, I'm going . . ."

"But to which one?" roared Dad.

"I'll know after tomorrow."

"Look here Debbie, you are still under age. You know what that means—you have to do what you're told."

"I'll telephone you tomorrow. I promise. Eight o'clock at the latest. Okay?"

"I hate okay. What does your mother say?"

"She wants me to go to school in London." My head was like a furnace now. I wanted to be left alone.

"I'll let you know tomorrow Dad . . . I promise." I put down the receiver slowly.

"Relax," Simon said. "If you don't you'll be in a devil of a mess tomorrow."

"Thank you for telling me."

I went outside and walked round the horses slowly. I thought, some of these stables have stood up for two hundred years; what does tomorrow matter by comparison. In two hundred years who will care whether I fall off or stay on. I thought, have a sense of proportion, pull yourself together. Cleo whinnied to me and I leaned over her box and told her that she was the best friend I had ever had. But she looked different now with her mane and tail pulled, her fetlocks gone, her coat as clean and gleaming as Rosie could make it. Her whiskers had gone too, but her feed was still in the manger uneaten. "You know then," I said. "You know about tomorrow. Don't worry."

The trailer was parked ready. My tack gleamed in the tack room and there were seven needles ready threaded with grey thread beside a comb and a pair of scissors on the table. Nothing was being left to chance.

"Hot chocolate?" offered Tina when I returned inside. "Ovaltine?"

"No thank you."

"Give her some whisky," said Simon.

"Ugh, no thank you."

My clothes were ready on a chair. I had a long hot bath and climbed into bed. It was dark outside now, but the air was full of rustling sounds. Birds were settling into nests, horses munching, rabbits cropping the fields. A lonely bird cried in the sky. I thought about the animals outside, about the peace of the countryside; but all the time, deeper than my thoughts, deeper than anything lurked tomorrow.

I thought, I'll let her choose her own pace. I'll just push her on if she needs it. I won't rush her. And I must listen for the starting bell and ride through the finish.

And then I slept at last and dreamed that I was starting at a new school. Mum wanted me to go to one classroom and Dad to another. They each pulled me one way and then suddenly it wasn't them pulling any more, but me pulling Cleo. I shouted, "Come on," and wakened to find that it was morning and that Tina was by my bed shouting, "Wake up, it's the Show today," and pulling at my bedclothes.

"Is it today?" I cried sitting up. "Is it Saturday? What's the time?"

"Eight o'clock. Cleo's ready. She looks marvellous. She's plaited up, everything. We didn't want to wake you too early. Breakfast is ready downstairs."

I had wanted to get her ready myself, to hold her while she was plaited, but it was too late now.

"And here's a letter."

It was from Mum. Inside was a cheque for five hundred pounds. 'It's the best I can do until next week,' she wrote. 'Can you put it down on Cleo, say you'll pay more later. I do hope so. And what about school. We must decide something. I'll come down on Sunday. I will ring up from the station when I get there, until then much love, Mum.'

PS 'Tell Simon I'm coming. I'll bring a contribution for lunch.'

106

I put the letter back into the envelope along with the cheque. It can keep until this evening I thought. Until I'm home again. Tina had put out her best shirt for me and a striped tie.

I could hear Derek swearing at a horse and Rosie running the yard tap. I felt pampered and I didn't like the feeling.

"Hurry up, we're loading Cleo," Simon yelled up the stairs.

Tying the tie for the third time, I thought, I never wanted to be special, I just wanted Cleo to compete at little shows for fun. I don't mind about never being famous . . .

I was ready now. I forced myself to eat breakfast. "I'm going to be your groom," said Tina.

I didn't want a groom either. I wanted to look after Cleo myself. I knew that the tables were turned now. Six weeks ago I was groom to Simon. It was a ridiculous situation.

Cleo whinnied to me from the trailer. She looked marvellous. "She's too good for me," I muttered climbing into the Land Rover.

"You made her what she is," Tina answered.

"Good luck," shouted Derek.

"Bring home a rosette," called Rosie from beneath a horse she was grooming.

The yard had never looked lovelier, the bricks were weathered, the window frames gleamed white and over everything hung that wonderful smell of horse and hay. I felt as though I was going to the scaffold, as though I would never come back.

"Do cheer up. If you do badly it's not the end of the

world," said Tina. "Some people would give everything they had to be you at this moment."

"She'll be all right when she gets there. She's got the Ravenswood nerve," said Simon.

"Have some chocolate," offered Tina.

"I've only just had breakfast ."

"The jumps will be only three foot three to begin with. It's a novice class," said Simon.

I bit my nails and looked out of the window. There was sunlight everywhere and the combine harvesters were already at work in the fields. "I just feel weak," I said. "Will I be in the main ring?"

Simon nodded. "It's an affiliated class. I've registered Cleo. Everyone will be out looking for promising young jumpers."

His words hardly registered. If they had, I might have refused to go on, for I still saw my future with Cleo, win or lose.

We stopped to fill up with petrol. It already seemed years since that disastrous drive with Derek and yet it was only a matter of weeks. Everything had taken place in one single holiday. Yet it seemed as though years had passed since I had said goodbye to our town house and joined Simon in this same Land Rover. And now my life at Bullrock seemed my normal life. It was almost as though I had always lived there. Tina passed round mugs of coffee. We reached a notice saying, TO THE SHOW, and my legs felt weaker than ever and I had butterflies in my stomach.

We passed another trailer and three horse boxes and Tina said, "Must you drive so fast. There's loads of time." I could see the tenseness in Simon now and I wanted to cry, "I'm not going through with it. I'm not good enough. Find someone else to ride for you."

But the words wouldn't come and now we were driving through a town, full of Saturday shoppers, pushing prams, carrying bags, holding each other's arms or walking alone. And I wished that I was with them. That I could be anonymous too, just someone walking in a crowd.

We turned left when we were out of the town and the Show lay before us like a picture—tents and stands, three rings, trailers, Land Rovers, pens of sheep and cattle, lines of gleaming new tractors.

There were thousands of cars parked on the hillside, and ponies in a ring, and foals prancing beside their mothers like toys.

I heard Cleo whinny in the trailer and I could feel Simon looking at me, as though he was summing me up for the first time, thinking "Can she do it?"

"It's only my second show," I said as though in answer. "I'll do my best, but you should have found someone better."

Tina squeezed my arm, "You'll be all right," she said. "I promise."

CHAPTER ELEVEN

We fetched my number. There were four people sitting behind a trestle table in a long tent. Most of them seemed to know Simon.

"She's my little sister," he said pointing at me. "She's riding for Bullrock today."

Next, we walked the course, because nothing had started yet in the main ring, though the stands were filling up already in anticipation. "Yours is the first class," Simon said. "But you're going late, so don't worry."

He told me how to ride each jump. "Don't rush the mare," he said. "Give her plenty of time, don't cut the corners either. You can leave that for the jump off against the clock."

"I shall never make that," I answered.

The combination was the worst jump. It ended with a triple. "You'll have to push on at that," Simon said. "And don't lose your nerve and do what you did last time, or I'll never speak to you again."

"What did I do?"

"The time you fell off," Simon replied slowly, "You gave up on the approach, you suddenly stopped everything, lost contact with hands and legs, and Cleo thought, what the heck is going on? And that was it. She hesitated just long enough to lose her stride. Keep contact Debbie, don't throw your reins away—ever."

Other competitors were in the ring now. Mostly groups of children walking round together, chatting and laughing saying things like, "Smokey will never do that," and "Wow, look at that wall." The more experienced ones measured out the combination in a proud, professional manner and I knew they had been competing at shows for years because people called to them from the ringside; "Are you going to win today?" "What are you riding then? Have you got a new one?"

And I wished that I could look professional too.

Simon legged me up. Tina pulled off the tail bandages. The first competitor was in the ring now and the judges in their glass box.

Simon pulled up my girths. "Trot her round. Let her look at everything," Simon said.

My legs felt like chewed string. "Don't look so miserable," Tina called. "It's meant to be fun."

I could see Bill Turpin now. He stood back and watched Cleo pass. Then he went across to Simon and I heard him ask "Do you know who owns the grey mare?"

Cleo shied at everything, then slowly she started to settle down and as her stride steadied, I felt my confidence coming back.

I started to canter and I thought, she can do it, there's nothing in the ring she can't do. It's simple. There's nothing to it, nothing at all.

Smokey, a blue roan was eliminated. A bay went in next, ridden by one of the professionals and jumped a

111

faultless round. Simon checked my girths again. "You had better get down to the collecting ring now," he said.

"What did Bill Turpin want?" I asked.

"Nothing special," replied my brother without looking at me.

"Is she going all right?" called Tina.

"Yes. She's fantastic," I replied, suddenly feeling as though my heart was breaking. They were calling my number now. Simon and Tina were making their way to the stands. I was alone with Cleo. No-one would tell me anything more. It was up to us.

Cleo was eager but calm at the same time. I had never loved her so much as I did at this moment. She seemed so dauntless and yet ready to give her all without question.

A steward in a hat said, "Are you ready? You're next."

I nodded, pushing my skull-cap down more firmly on my head, thinking how far away London seemed and now many years ago was yesterday. The competitor ahead of me came out to a burst of clapping. Delighted parents rushed towards him calling, "Well done, Jeremy. Jolly good," as though they had expected three refusals.

Then I was alone in the ring with Cleo, cantering a circle, my nervousness completely gone. I didn't look at the stands. I thought, there's plenty of time, Debbie, all the time in the world. Then the bell went and I cantered on steadily towards the first jump and we popped over as though it was nothing.

I heard the announcer give my name as I rode on

towards the wall, and for one awful moment I thought that Cleo was going to run out, then we were over that too, cantering on towards the third jump, and I began to enjoy myself. I remembered Simon's words as I rode towards the combination. I kept contact and pushed on towards the triple and Cleo lengthened her stride and cocked her ears. I could feel her mind working as we jumped, one, two, three, to a tremendous burst of clapping and then we turned sharp right and cantered on to the road closed; the wall which followed looked larger than it was, but Cleo didn't hesitate, and now there were only three jumps left and neither of us was blown or tired, just going on as steady as a rock. I wasn't really concentrating any more and then I heard Simon's voice clearly from the stands crying in exasperation, "She isn't concentrating any more. She's going the wrong way," and I pulled myself together and turned swiftly for the oxer, the crossed bars and the last spread. Then we were over all three and the honour of the stables was still intact.

"I thought you were going to sleep," shouted Simon rushing from the stands. "Anyway, it was a clear round."

"Now for the jump off," said Tina loosening Cleo's girths.

We watched the jumps go up to three foot six and it didn't look like a novice class any more.

"There's five of you to jump off and they're getting short of time," Simon said.

"The triple looks enormous, and just look at the oxer!" I cried.

"You'll be all right," Tina said.

"Don't lose your nerve. She can do it," said Simon, legging me up.

I was the last to go. There was only one clear round when my turn came. A brown pony had been eliminated and a dun with a Roman nose had had four faults.

"Ride like you did last time," said Simon.

"I'll do my best."

We went in calmly. In the distance a child was crying and somewhere a cow was lowing. There was a babble of voices from the stands, which hushed as I rode in.

The bell went almost at once. I heard someone say, "She's a newcomer," as I rode towards the first jump. And then it was just me and Cleo again alone in the ring.

Cleo jumped the first marvellously and the second. I thought of Tina and Simon up in the stands and how much it mattered to them, and then all too soon we were riding towards the dreaded combination. Cleo cleared the first part easily, she was a little wrong for the second, but she tucked her legs up under her and we were clear, and then with one stirrup missing I pushed on towards the triple. She lengthened her stride and took off too close, and I felt my other stirrup go as she soared into the air. I thought I heard a groan, but probably it was simply my imagination. I tried to grab her mane but now we were landing and I was pitching forward with her, my balance completely gone, and there seemed to be a great silence as the crowd waited. I was still hang-

114

ing on when we turned for the oxer and I think Simon screamed, "Stay on Debbie," though I can't be sure because everything happened so quickly. Cleo cantered on towards the oxer with my arms round her neck and the reins dangling by her knees. And then, without warning, my strength failed me. I let go and felt the ground come up to meet me, and hit my shoulders.

The crowd clapped me as I stood up. A steward led Cleo towards me.

"Do you want to go on?" he asked. "You don't have to." I nodded brushing grass from my knees. He straightened the saddle. I mounted and rode on over the oxer and then over the other two jumps to a tremendous burst of clapping.

"You're third," cried Tina. "Well done!"

I looked for disappointment on their faces, but they were both smiling.

"I let Cleo down. I'm sorry," I said.

"You did your best. No-one can do more than that," said my brother.

My number was being called now. I rode in with a girl and a boy with fair hair. A lady wearing a big hat handed us our rosettes. A band started to play as we cantered round the ring.

As we rode out the girl said, "I'm buying your pony. Dad's paying anything you ask. It's all arranged."

I said, "You must be mad," while my heart hammered against my ribs. "She's not for sale!"

"You can ask your brother. I'm going to be Junior Champion of Europe when I'm older. It's all settled," she replied.

115

I dismounted slowly. "What's this about Cleo going?" I asked Tina. "She didn't jump a clear round in the jump off. She can still improve."

Tina looked at me and then away. "The girl who won says her Dad's buying her," I said in an accusing voice which shook slightly.

"You had better ask Simon," Tina replied.

I handed Cleo to Tina and went in search of my brother. I remembered Mum's cheque. Suddenly I was glad that I had fallen off, it made Cleo worth less.

I started to run and nearly fell over a little girl eating an ice cream. The band was still playing. The sun was shining. I ran through a crowd of horses. I stopped, my eyes searching the horse boxes. I ran to the Land Rover. Simon wasn't there so I went back to Tina.

"Where is he?" I asked. "I must know. I want to buy Cleo."

"He's probably in the bar. Take Cleo to the trailer and untack her. I'll find him."

I rode Cleo across to the trailer thinking about the girl with the plait and wondering whether her father was very rich. I untacked Cleo, watered her and let her graze—and waited. Time seemed to pass very slowly now. I wondered whether Simon was making a deal at this very moment. I felt panic fomenting inside me until I wanted to scream. Then I saw Tina approaching. "He's just coming," she called.

"I want to buy Cleo," I shouted. "I've got some money."

"Yes, all right," replied Tina in a soothing voice as though I was ill.

116

"Mum sent me some this morning. Dad will let me have some more. I want to buy her, I'm making an offer now."

"We must wait for Simon," replied Tina, her face worried, her hands clasped together as though she was praying for patience.

"I trained her," I cried. "No-one could ride her before, don't you remember?" I was shouting now, and people were looking.

"I know. You've been marvellous," Tina said.

But I didn't want praise. I wanted Cleo. Nothing else was enough.

"I'll pay five thousand pounds, six. She was only worth three when I came, please Tina," I said. I could feel tears coming and I was too old to cry. "I'll work for you for years for nothing."

"Yes, I know. I'm so grateful to you," Tina replied. "You've no idea."

"You're putting it on, you're not grateful. No-one is," I cried. "I hate that girl with the plait," I shouted. "She's a horrible child. I wish, I wish . . . I wish she would fall off and break her neck."

Tina poured me a mug of coffee. "Calm down. Everyone's looking."

My brother was coming now. He looked tall and handsome and he was smiling.

I wanted to shout, "Is she sold?" but the words wouldn't come, so instead, I called, "I want to buy Cleo. I'm offering you five thousand pounds."

My brother raised his eyebrows. "You're too late," he said.

"Six," I shouted. "Seven . . ."

"She's sold," he said. "I'm sorry. I didn't want to sell her; but I had to."

"I hate you," I shouted. "I hate that girl with the plait. I hate everyone."

"You will have your reward," replied Simon.

"I don't want a reward. I want Cleo," I shouted.

"I couldn't refuse," explained Simon. "The offer was too large. Mr Hopkins has been looking for a good jumper for some time. He's very ambitious for his daughter. He wants her to go to the top. He's ready to spend huge sums to that end. He's just sold some land for two million, so money is no object as the saying goes."

I felt very cold now. I led Cleo into the trailer.

"To cut a long story short, he's paying twenty thousand for Cleo," said my brother throwing up the ramp.

CHAPTER TWELVE

I didn't speak on the way home. I felt completely numb. I looked out of the window and saw nothing. Money always wins, I thought.

I decided that I would leave Bullrock in the morning and never return. I was completely exhausted. My sleepless nights had taken their toll. When Tina spoke to me I refused to answer. I heard Simon say, "Leave her alone. She'll get over it."

And I vowed that I would never speak to either of them again.

"Would you like an ice cream?" asked Tina.

I shook my head. I'm not a child, I thought, to be consoled with ice cream.

"Is it money you want?" asked Simon at last.

I shook my head. "I hate money," I muttered.

I thought of the girl with a plait riding Cleo, schooling her. I imagined a groom washing Cleo, plaiting her mane. I imagined a long line of rosettes hanging on a wall and Cleo growing older, whiter. I looked at Simon and despised him, because he put money first. We were nearly home how. It was afternoon. Cows were being driven towards their hygienic milking parlours. I'm going to live in London. I'm never coming back, I decided.

Derek and Rosie were waiting, listening for the

sound of the Land Rover. Spick and Span were waiting too. The yard had shadows across it.

"How did you do?" called Derek. "Did you win?"

My face was tearstained. I jumped out of the Land Rover and ran into the cottage. I heard Tina say, "She's upset. We've sold Cleo."

And Derek's matter-of-fact reply, "I knew it would happen sooner or later."

I fled upstairs to my room. Nothing ever stays the same. And I haven't anything stable that I can call my own, I thought. I turned on my Walkman but music didn't mean anything to me. I could only see Cleo going away, her box empty next day.

I opened the window and I could hear the horses munching, and Rosie trundling the old barrow with the loose wheel. I heard Simon laugh and a horse kicking at his loose-box door and I could see Spick and Span chasing each other in mad circles while one of Rosie's brothers carried a hay-net. I hated myself for being miserable and I hated Simon.

I threw my Walkman across the room and started packing. I thought, I'll go back with Mum tomorrow and that will be that, and all the time I was crying because I didn't want to go.

Presently when I'd filled my suitcase, I heard a knock on the door and a voice saying, "Can I come in? It's me, Derek."

"I suppose so," I said pushing my hair out of my eyes.

"So you're packing," he exclaimed, looking at my suitcase. "I knew you would leave in the end. You're not tough enough, that's your trouble."

"They offered me money," I answered. "But I don't want it."

"London or Oxford?" inquired Derek.

"Why don't you go away! Leave my room! Get out!" I shouted.

"You didn't want me to leave Simon in the lurch and now you're doing it—surprise, surprise," exclaimed Derek.

"It's tea," shouted Tina. "Come down, Debbie. We want to talk to you."

"I'm not coming," I said. "I don't want to speak to you, not either of you. NOT ever again."

"Well, I'm going," said Derek and left the room slamming the door after him.

Later someone said, "Dinner, Debbie," and I heard a tray put down outside my door.

I waited until I heard footsteps going downstairs before I opened the door and took in the tray. There was a bowl of soup, brown bread, a lamb chop with mashed potato and cabbage, pineapple chunks. I tried to eat, but tears ran down my cheeks like a river and everything tasted salty. I wasn't crying for Cleo now, I was crying because I couldn't decide what to do, because I had no home. Suddenly all my hopes were dead. I felt as though the sun would never rise again. I left the tray in the passage, washed my face and prepared for bed. The yard was quiet; twilight had come, a lovely dreamy September twilight. The day's work was over. Outside Spick and Span were lying together in the dusk. Cleo was staring out of her box into the distance. I dried my eyes and looked at her. I thought, there will never

121

me another Cleo. Horses like her are born not made, and I climbed into bed very slowly as though I was old. I could hear a bird crying in the night sky, the one which always cried as though he was searching for something, and I thought, I feel like him. I've lost something too.

Next morning I got up early and hurried down to the stables. Derek was feeding and I started to muck out. I didn't want to speak to anyone and they didn't speak to me. I worked at great speed. I wanted them to miss me when I was gone, to say if only Debbie was still here. She did so much. I turned Cleo out without asking anyone. Then I made myself some toast and a mug of coffee and sat eating in my room, looking at the elms along the ridge, saying goodbye, because today I was leaving. I heard Simon say, " Catch up Cleo, Derek, she's going at two and I don't want her sent away covered with mud." And I pretended that I didn't care, that I was finished with horses. I heard Simon start the Land Rover and drive away. Then Tina called up the stairs. "Are you all right, Debbie? Have you got a headache? A temperature?"

"I'm all right, I'm packing," I shouted. And I shut my suitcase with a bang.

"What a pity, we'll miss you," Tina called.

"I'm going to get educated like you wanted," I shouted in a voice so bitter that I hardly knew it as my own. "I'm going to pass my exams and work in an office and I'm going to wear a skirt every day to work." But I knew it wasn't true, because I'm not capable of being a typist.

Then I heard the Land Rover coming back and presently Mum's voice saying, "Well where is she?" and then, "Debbie, come down."

I went down the stairs slowly. I wanted to appear hurt but dignified.

Mum called, "Come on Debbie, I hear you were marvellous yesterday. You rode like a dream, and we're in the money again. Hurry, darling. I've got lots to tell you."

I jumped the last two stairs and Mum kissed me while Tina appeared carrying cups of coffee.

"Yes, she was fabulous," she said. "I've never seen anyone learn anything as quickly as Debbie. She's the fastest mucker- out at Bullrock."

"We have a proposal to make, my brother said in a sober voice. "Will you all sit down?"

And I saw that there were chairs round the sitting room table and a pad of paper waiting to be written on.

"Simon and Tina sat one at each end while I sat on my brother's left and Mum on his right. I wanted to say, "What is all this?" but, since I still wasn't speaking to Tina and Simon, I couldn't.

"It's about the money we got for Cleo," my brother said. "We want Debbie to have a share in it. We wanted to talk to her about it last night, but she was hating us all too much."

He was talking about me as though I wasn't there, but suddenly I didn't mind. He turned to look at me for the first time in hours. "We want you to be a director," he said.

"A director? A director of what?" I cried.

"We want you to have a share in this business," Tina explained. "We don't want to lose you."

"We are going to form a company," my brother said. "The Bullrock Stables Ltd. We reckon Cleo was worth four thousand and the other sixteen thousand is partly yours, Debbie, because you made her what she is."

"We are going to build a covered school," Tina said. "And give lessons."

Their faces were lit up with excitement.

I imagined the covered school. I saw myself teaching, schooling young horses in it.

"This will be your home," said Tina looking into my face. "We will build you a room which will be yours with its own front door."

"You will have a third share," Simon told me. "The horses will all belong to the company, everything will."

My head seemed to be going round and round. I felt filled with guilt. All I could say was, "I'm sorry. I've been so awful."

"You can go to London if you want to," Tina said. "But you'll still have a third share, a share of the profits too, when there are some."

"I want to stay here," I answered, and my voice seemed to come from a long way off. "I want this to be my home. You don't really mind do you, Mum?"

I went to the window and looked at the yard and thought, a third of it is mine. It was impossible to realise, better than any dream, better than anything which had ever happened to me before.

I saw now why Simon had had to sell Cleo. If we

124

had a covered school, pupils could ride whatever the weather. We could have a jumping show every month and make money that way. We could keep the horses fit even when there was snow three feet deep outside.

"And the five hundred pounds is a gift to put down on a saddle you can call your own," Mum told me, her arm around my shoulder looking out of the window too.

"You will soon be out of children's classes," Simon said. "You need something bigger than Cleo, something you can school on for Horse Trials in two years' time."

He believed in me. I knew that now. It was like being given an enormous dish of something after you've been hungry a long time.

"Cleo will do better with a smaller child," Tina continued. Angela Hopkins is only eleven. She's going to be good, really good, and Cleo will be at her peak in two years' time. She will be able to upgrade her next year, and jump at Wembley the year after."

I imagined myself watching Cleo jump on television. And then one day I would be at Wembley too.

"We must fix up school," Mum said moving away from the window. I told them that I wanted to go to the local school. "I want to make friends with local people of my own age. And ride in the evenings after school. I can't do that if I go away to somewhere smart . . ."

"As long as you are sure," Mum said, "because I've got news too—I'm marrying again."

I said, "Oh, Mum."

And Simon said quickly, "It's the best thing, a fresh start."

"Yes, it is," agreed Tina.

I thought of Dad among his books in Oxford, but I didn't say anything. I thought he'll probably re-marry himself soon, grown ups are very unpredictable, even one's parents.

We walked round the horses before lunch and I kept thinking, a third of this is mine and it still seemed impossible.

We had a roast lunch, Simon opened a bottle of wine and we all drank toasts to THE BULLROCK STABLES LTD. Then we sat and talked until there was a knock on the door and Simon cried, "Good lord, it's the Hopkins come for Cleo."

He smoothed his hair down and put on boots and we all went outside into the swept silent yard. Cleo's head still pulled at my heartstrings but today Angela seemed much nicer. She kept patting Cleo and she said, "I'm going to keep her for ever and ever. And you can come and see her whenever you like, can't she Dad?"

Mr Hopkins smoked a cigar, and he called Cleo, "My little darling."

"Yes, any time," he said. "You'll always be wel-come."

I could feel a lump rising in my throat as Simon led Cleo out of her box; she looked so lovely. Mr Hopkins put on a summer sheet while Angela and I adjusted knee caps over her neat grey knees. I kissed her under her mane and then Simon led her up the ramp while I gulped back tears.

"We'll send you a photograph of her with Angy up," said Mr Hopkins, "Won't we, Angy?"

Angy nodded. "She'll be all right with us. We've got a super girl groom," she said.

"Angy's ponies have everything," said Mr Hopkins with pride. "Nothing is too good for them."

The ramp was up now, the bolts turned, Mr Hopkins and Simon shook hands. Rosie was just starting to do evening stables. I couldn't see Cleo any more now.

"Be seeing you," Angy said climbing into the Land Rover. "Perhaps," I said suddenly knowing that anything was possible now, absolutely anything . . .

I started to muck out Cleo's empty box and I thought, tomorrow I won't care so much, and Tina is right, I would have been too big for her next year . . .

Presently it was tea time and Mum said, "I must be going soon. When shall I see you again?"

I said that I didn't know and she said that she would come down herself again then. So we all sat round the table once more drinking tea, and I felt happy for the first time in days in a deep, satisfying sort of way. I felt secure at last and I knew the happiness would last. Although there would never be another Cleo, there would be another horse, perhaps a braver horse, though I doubted it.

We all rode in the Land Rover to the station. The terriers yapped wildly in the back and Simon whistled and I saw that Mum was happy too. We waited till the train had gone and then we rushed back to the stables and Simon said, "Let's decide where the school will be, and what about your private bedsitting room, Debbie?"

And Tina said, "We've got to find her a horse."

"We must draw up legal documents too," added Simon. "I'll see the solicitor in the morning."

"I would like a grey or a dun or failing that, a roan," I said, and I saw a cavalcade of horses, roans and greys and duns until finally one would be mine until it died, beyond price.

"We'll have a gallery," said Simon and there'll be heating for the spectators and perhaps a changing room. We must think big, Tina."

Tina nodded and Spick and Span started tearing backwards and forwards, asking for their supper. I thought, this is really home now; no-one can take it away, and that was the best thing of all.